Chapel Bend

A Huckleberry Bay novel

Kristen Proby

AMPERSAND
PUBLISHING, INC.

Chapel Bend
A Huckleberry Bay Novel
By
Kristen Proby

CHAPEL BEND

A Huckleberry Bay Novel

Cover Design: By Hang Le

Cover photo: Wander Aguiar

This one is for me. Every word of this book was a delight to write. It made me laugh, and it made me cry. And it reminded me that I was once a young girl who dreamed of doing this job for the joy of it, first and foremost. I love this story, and I'm grateful to you for reading it.

Prologue

June

Januany 1, 2000

DEAR DIARY,

Well, here we are. I don't really know what to write, but I promised Luna and Sarah that, as of today, I'd start keeping a diary with them. We found a really old leather book up in the lighthouse a couple of weeks ago that turned out to be a journal from some old lady, and I guess it's kind of cool. Luna only wants to read it when the three of us are together, one journal entry at a time, so it'll take us about thirty years to read it all, but that's okay.

I just don't know what to say. I mean, I'm only thirteen years old, and there's not much of anything interesting going on. Well, I guess that isn't true.

1

Apollo pissed me off. Again.

Here's hoping my grandma doesn't find this because she'd twist my ear for swearing. She says a lady shouldn't use such language, but I hear her swear all the time. And, besides, I'm no lady. We all know it.

Anyway, Apollo is a jerk. He may be Luna's big brother, and she loves him because he's related to her, but he can suck it. I think he makes it his life's ambition to hurt my feelings. He may be named after a god, and he definitely looks like one, but he's an ass. I can't believe that I ever had a crush on him. He humiliated me! So, now, he gets my wrath for all eternity.

Lucky him.

Oh, and I get to start woodshop this semester at school. I'm really excited. I like to build things. I know that the boys all sneer at me, but I'm way better at it than they are! They're just jealous. Losers. I'll show them. Girls can make stuff out of wood and fix cars and do whatever the hell we want.

Grandma's calling me down for dinner, so I better go. I guess I'll see you tomorrow.

-Juniper

Chapter One

June

"Now, that is *pretty*."

With my hands on my hips, I stand on the sidewalk in front of the chapel that I bought six months ago and smile. The leaves in Huckleberry Bay are starting to turn with the change of summer into fall, flanking my freshly painted white building with orange and red and yellow. It's *gorgeous*.

The smell of salt from the ocean, which is less than a mile away, is heavy in the air, and I tilt my head up to the sunshine, close my eyes, and take a long, deep breath.

I love the sunshine, the bright blue sky, and most of all, I love that my schedule is finally lightening up enough that I can spend time renovating my own place rather than working on other construction projects.

Not that I'm complaining about the work. I'm grateful that the small construction company I started a few years ago has taken off as well as it has. But I'm dying to really dig into this chapel and rehab it into my own home.

"Nice paint job."

My eyes open at the sound of the voice that never fails to make my knees weak, but before I turn to Apollo Winchester, I school my face into just this side of a snarl.

"What are you doing here?"

He doesn't scowl. He doesn't look confused. He just grins.

"You invited me, remember?"

"I must have been psychotic at the time because I can guaran-damn-tee you that I didn't invite you to my home." Of course, I did. I just don't know how to interact with Apollo without giving him a hard time.

"You need me." He pauses, a smirk still hovering over his sexy-as-sin lips before continuing, "To do your electrical."

Doesn't that just grate on the nerves? I'm going to have to run new electrical through the whole house, and Apollo is the best electrician in the county—maybe the state—and I won't settle for anything but the best when it comes to my place.

"Right." I roll my eyes and turn to walk up the steps to the double doors that lead into the chapel. Once I unlock the door, I push inside and take a deep breath. It smells a little musty and a little like saw dust. "Come on in, and I'll go over my plans with you."

"I can't wait."

I avoid eye contact as I turn on lights and then open a few of the windows to let in some fresh air.

"I haven't been here in about a week so it's stuffy."

It's one big room with a beautiful hardwood floor, which is original to the building, as well as a few wooden pews and an altar.

Those things will go or be repurposed, of course.

"No blood stain," Apollo murmurs and then raises his head to meet my gaze.

"No. I had a company come in and clean the blood."

He nods, and we're both thinking of Sarah, whose ex-husband almost killed her in this chapel six months ago. It was a terrifying day, but my dear friend is safe, and her ex is tucked away in a maximum-security prison, so we can all put that behind us.

"Some people wouldn't want to live in a place where something like that happened."

I frown and shake my head. "It's not the chapel's fault. Besides, Sarah didn't die, thank all the gods, and it was only a little blood to clean up. It's fine."

Apollo nods and looks around. "This is going to be really cool, Juniper."

God, I love the way he says my name, and I normally *hate* being called by my full name. Everyone calls me June.

But not Apollo.

No, he has to say my full name like it's sweetness on his tongue. He finds ways to slip it into conversation here and there, and it slides along my nerves like warm honey. Which only irritates me.

Unfortunately, after a night of bad decisions three months ago, I know exactly what it sounds like when he says my name in the middle of some mind-numbing sex, and I don't think I'll ever fully recover from that. Why, oh why, did I have to give in to temptation and accept his offer of going home with him at the bar that night? I wasn't *that* drunk.

Except, I know why. It's because the chemistry between us, despite my ferocious disdain for him, is off the charts, and I thought I could work him out of my system.

It didn't work.

"Juniper."

I blink and raise my eyebrows. "Sorry, what?"

He studies me with narrowed eyes. "What were you thinking about?"

"How annoying you are. What did you say?"

"How many rooms are you going to frame in?"

"Two bedrooms, one and a half baths." I walk around, pointing out where I picture everything going. "There's an office through that door that I'm going to turn into a laundry and mud room. And there's a basement, but I don't know what I'm going to do with it."

"There's a basement?" He sounds surprised, but then he nods and shoves his hands into his pockets. The movement makes the muscles in his arms and chest flex, and I have to take a long, slow breath. "That's right. I've seen the small windows in the foundation. That'll be good because we can run most of the wiring down. That'll work for plumbing, too. Who do you have doing that?"

"Maxwell Tilly."

Apollo nods in satisfaction. Max does a great job, and I was lucky that he could fit me into his schedule.

"Are you replacing the stained glass?"

Behind the altar there is a beautiful, arched piece of stained glass featuring Jesus on the cross. On each of the two walls perpendicular to that one, there are five more windows that display different scenes from the Bible.

"Yes. I thought long and hard about it, but I need more light. Not to mention, I absolutely don't want Jesus watching every move I make, you know?"

"I can understand that. What are you going to do with them?"

"I'm selling them to a church in Portland who's building a new place. They were excited to get these windows since they're antique, and the artistry is really beautiful."

"That's a good idea."

"I didn't want them to get chucked. So, I'm glad they're going to a new home. They should have a crew out here to take them out next week."

"That soon?"

"Yeah. I'm ready to get going on this project, Apollo."

"I don't blame you. Okay, well, I'll have an estimate written up and sent over to you in the next couple of days. I can work in stages as you get things done. I know that's not usually how we do it, but I think that once you get your hands into this, it's going to go quickly."

"That's my hope. I'm still finishing things up over at the inn. Luna's been impatient and disappointed that we hit some snafus." I sigh. "There was way more outside work than I anticipated, and there was nothing I could do about it."

"Luna's fine," he assures me. "My sister's a smart woman, and she understands what delays and back orders on products can do to a project. Besides, she gets to have her big, fancy opening in time for Christmas, so she's excited about that."

"I am, too." I nod and look around the room once more. "I'm hoping to be living *here* by Christmas."

"Whoa. It's the middle of October."

"Yep." I turn to him and offer him a bright smile. "So, we'd better get busy."

Apollo's phone rings at the same time as mine does, and when I check mine, I see it's my crew at the inn.

"I'd better get back to work."

"Me, too," he replies. "I'll be in touch about the estimate."

"Thanks."

He pulls up short and narrows his eyes at me.

"What?"

"You just *thanked* me. Do you have a fever?"

Now, my back is up, and I feel bristly. "Because I'm a fucking *professional*, Apollo. Now, get out of my chapel."

"That's more like it," he decides with a nod and walks out ahead of me. I leave the windows open to let the place air out some more, but I make sure the door is locked before I walk to my truck.

Apollo is standing by his own truck, watching me with dark eyes that roam up and down my body.

"What?"

"Are we ever going to talk about it?"

"About what?" I'm not oblivious. I know what he's referring to. An amazing night of sweaty sex and laughter and about twelve hours of truce where we did nothing but enjoy each other.

The next morning, he was gone, and we were back to our normal relationship.

"You know what."

"I'm not going to stand here and play games with you. I have a job to do."

I move to open the door of my truck, but Apollo jogs over to me, pushes the door closed, and pins me against the side.

"Pushy much?"

"You know damn well what I'm talking about."

Against my will, my eyes drop to his lips. I can't help it. They're so firm and hot, and they did things to me that I didn't know existed outside of romance novels.

But they do. They *so* do.

"We're not going to talk about it," I whisper, still looking at those lips. "Not ever. We agreed on that at the time, and you know it."

"Yeah, well, I've reconsidered."

"No." My eyes meet his now. "You don't get to change the rules just because you have an itch to scratch. I didn't agree to be your friend with benefits, Apollo."

"That's not—"

"I have to get to work."

I push him away and get into my truck. With all of

the will in my body, I do *not* look out the window at him as I start the engine and drive away.

It isn't until I've hit the end of the drive that I relent and allow myself one glance in the rearview. Apollo is still standing there with his hands on his hips and a scowl on that magnificent face as he stares after me.

I never promised him *anything*. In fact, before I even left the bar with him that night, we had agreed that nothing would change and that it would be just one night of sex. That's it. No promises.

Now that it's been a few months, he wants to talk about it? Unacceptable.

Absolutely *not*.

We've gone back to disliking each other, which is exactly the way it should be.

Shaking off that altercation with the annoyingly sexy Apollo, I roll down my window, take a deep breath, and shake it off.

Huckleberry Bay is quiet today. It's a weekday, and we're finally outside of the heart of the tourist season, so I can drive through town without having to find a back road to avoid delays. I love that I can see the ocean as I drive through town, and when I glance toward it, I can make out a few people on the beach with kites.

While it might be a sunny day, it's not calm. We always have wind here on the ocean.

Before long, I'm through town and on my way up Lighthouse Way, the long road that leads up to the light-house and Luna's new inn. I pass by her husband's personal garage and see that two of the big doors are up and cars are being worked on in there.

Wolfe was a successful racecar driver for a long time, but last year, he was injured and had to retire. So, he came home to heal from his injuries and fell in love with Luna.

I can't blame him. Luna's damn lovable. She and Sarah have been my best friends since kindergarten.

As I drive up the hill, the lighthouse comes into view first, but then I can see the inn. It used to be an old barn on the property that hadn't been used in many years, but we are almost finished remodeling it into a gorgeous bed-and-breakfast.

It should be open already, but I ran into problem after problem this summer with everything from landscapers to stonemasons to finishing carpenters. I laid my first patio all on my own because I was told that I'd have to wait for spring.

No way, no how.

Luna's had to wait long enough as it is, and I wasn't going to ask her to wait until spring for the patio off the gorgeous kitchen to be finished.

All that aside, it's all finally coming together, and Luna should be ready for customers by November first.

Just in time for the holidays.

She's often said that she wants to throw big, lavish holiday parties at the inn and invite everyone in Huckleberry Bay to attend. This year, that can happen, and I can't wait to see how she dresses the place up.

I park under the little portico in front of the entrance

of Luna's Light and cut the engine, frowning when I see Wally, my finishing carpenter, leaning against a column.

"Shouldn't you be *inside*?"

"It's happening again." His jaw tightens, and then he swears under his breath. "It's damn unnerving, June."

"Do you smell the roses?"

"That, *and* the doors have been shutting themselves and then opening back up again. I never agreed to work with a ghost."

"I get it. Having Rose around can be disconcerting."

"That's one way to put it."

I take a deep breath. I don't want to lose Wally, so telling him to man up and tell the ghost to take a hike probably isn't the best solution here.

"Let me see what I can do."

I walk inside and hear some hammering upstairs as well as some movement in the small dining room.

Then I smell the roses.

I know for a fact that Luna hasn't started the weekly flower deliveries yet, so this is all Rose, the ghost of a woman who died about a hundred and fifty years ago.

"Rose," I say firmly, trying to sound authoritative. "I need you to stop scaring the workers. I know that you've saved our butts in the past, but I promise you that there's no danger here to anyone. We need to finish up so Luna can finally open for business."

"People would be nuts to stay here," Wally mutters behind me, and he's answered by a loud slamming door upstairs.

"Okay." I whirl around and scowl at Wally. "I get that

she scares you. I'm sorry about that, but we are *almost* finished. If you just put in some earbuds or something and ignore her, you'll be all finished by the end of the week, and you never have to step foot in here again. She won't hurt you. Please don't quit."

"Thought about it," he admits. "The music isn't a bad idea. I'll try that."

"Good. Thank you." I turn back toward the stairs. "Hear that, Rose? He's going to make an effort. I'd appreciate it if you would do the same."

"Does she bug everyone like this?"

"Actually, no. I wonder why she doesn't like you?"

Wally sighs and shifts from foot to foot. "I think I know."

"Enlighten me."

He clears his throat while he eyes the stairs. "My great-grandpa worked for her and did some repairs on the lighthouse and stuff. Maybe she didn't like him."

Another slam.

"Looks like you've hit the nail on the head." I shake my head. "Get over it, Rose. Wally isn't his great-grandpa. Please be nice to him." Then I pat Wally's shoulder. "Thanks for hanging in there."

He nods. "I'm going to go find those earbuds."

While he does that, I walk through to the kitchen and smile to myself. The inn gleams in beautiful, polished walnut and smells of freshly baked cookies.

"You're just in time," Luna says and gestures to Mira, who's pulling out two baking trays from the industrial wall oven.

"I love it when I have good timing."

"I'm also baking a pie," Mira says with a wink. "So, save room."

"You won't get any argument out of me. How are things at the restaurant?"

Three Sisters Kitchen is owned by Mira and her two sisters, Cordelia and Darla. They also bought into the kitchen side of this inn with Luna, so I know the three of them have to be incredibly busy.

"Hopping," she says with a laugh and uses a towel to wipe at a little sweat on her forehead. "We hired two new chefs, and even though we haven't opened here yet, I suspect I'll need to hire more."

"Not a bad problem to have." I reach for a fresh chocolate chip cookie, take a bite, then sigh in absolute happiness. "So good."

"*So* good," Luna agrees and takes another bite of her own cookie. "How are you? Did you meet with my brother at the chapel?"

"Yeah." The mention of Apollo almost ruins the cookie for me. Almost. "He annoys the hell out of me, but we'll get everything worked out. In the meantime, I'm overseeing the wrap-up on this place, and then I'll dig into my own."

"We got the okay on the kitchen, plumbing, and electrical from the county," Luna informs me, but when I just grin, she rolls her eyes. "You already know that."

"I'm the contractor. Of course, I know. The health department will be back to do a final walk-through once everything is done."

"It's all coming together," Mira says with a happy sigh. "At last."

"I know it took longer than planned." I pop the rest of the cookie into my mouth. "And I'm sorry for it, but I wanted it all done *right*."

"Honestly, I think it's happening right when it's supposed to," Luna replies. "Besides, I wasn't ever mad *at* you so much as a little disappointed and frustrated *for* you, so there is no need to apologize. I'm going to take reservations from locals so they have a chance to stay here free of charge and experience it before I open it up to vacationers. Kind of like a soft opening."

"I think that's smart." I nod, thinking it over. "Many of those people own businesses that cater to tourists, so it would be great marketing. If they love it, which we all know they will, they'll recommend the inn to their customers."

"Agreed," Mira adds. "And I think it's good morale for the community. They're so excited about this inn, and making them feel like they're part of it will give them a sense of pride in its success."

"I'm honestly relieved that they *are* excited," Luna admits. "They could have gone the other way and been angry about another tourist trap in town."

"I haven't heard anyone say anything bad about that," I reply. "Granted, I'm the one building it, so maybe they wouldn't say anything to me directly, but my grandma keeps her ear to the ground, and she hasn't heard anything either."

"Good." Luna sighs in relief. "I'm so excited, you

guys. Oh, and the holiday décor is coming in two weeks. It's *stunning*."

"Will you put a real Christmas tree in the foyer?"

"Of course." She grins. "Wolfe and I plan to go cut one down the day after Thanksgiving."

"Epic," Mira declares. "This place is going to be *epic*."

"You bet your ass it is," I reply and reach for another cookie.

JUNE 14, 2010

Dear Diary,

My construction business is finally open! All of the ridiculous paperwork is filed with the state. I have permits and certificates and licenses coming out my ears, and I can finally put all of my hard work to...well, WORK. I'm finally done killing myself for the sake of someone else's business, making a measly hourly wage.

I haven't had as much pushback from some of the "good ol' boys" as I expected, which is a relief. In fact, I didn't have a problem at all finding enough people for a full crew. I know that guys will come and go, and that's okay, but I'm just so freaking excited to have my own business. I'm going to make it work if it's the last thing I do.

Grandma is my first client. She wants me to build a new deck for her, so that's where we're starting.

I have some possible projects lined up for the summer, too. Here's hoping I stay busy! I now have a crew to pay, insurance to pay, and all kinds of other things that you don't think about.

Luna and I are going to celebrate with pizza and beer at Lighthouse Pizza. I wish Sarah was here to celebrate with us. She'd get a huge kick out of it! I miss her. Don't tell anyone I said that. Because I'm also really, REALLY mad at her.

Anyway, here's to a new business! May it be awesome for a long, long time.

Xo,

June

Chapter Two

Apollo

I hate this house.

It's not horrible, and I've seen far worse, but this isn't the house that I'll grow old in.

Plopping onto the couch, I let out a long breath and take a pull from the beer I retrieved from the fridge. Not too long ago, my buddy Tanner pointed out that this place is *sad,* and he's right. I've lived here for over ten years and have yet to hang anything on the walls. It's cold and sterile, which has nothing to do with the thermostat, but it has the necessities, and that's really all I need for now. Besides, I'm hardly ever here. I live and breathe my job, and I spend a lot of time with my friends and family.

Basically, this is where I flop down and shower before going back to my life.

But, this evening, I'm too damn tired to care about the blank walls and boring décor of my house. It was a long day, and I spent a portion of it subcontracting out a couple of jobs so nothing gets lost in the shuffle or falls behind deadline.

The truth is, fitting June's project into my schedule was a pain in the ass, not that she'll ever know that. I'll help her—at cost—without a fucking word about the inconvenience because it's *June*.

She may give me a hard time and glare at me more than she's ever smiled at me, but at the end of the day, there isn't anything I wouldn't do for her. So, if she wants to live in that tiny church by Christmas, that's what will happen, come hell or high water.

My phone pings with a text, and I'm a little surprised to see that it's from Tanner. Since he and Sarah have been together again, I hear from him less, which is completely expected and normal.

TANNER: *Hey, feel like a beer and pizza?*
  I snort.
  Me: Do birds fly? Meet in 20?
  Tanner: See you there.

AFTER SETTING the almost-full beer back in the fridge, I change into clean clothes, grab my keys, and head out for dinner with a friend. Lighthouse Pizza is our favorite haunt in town, and I could go for a pie tonight.

The drive is short, and when I walk inside the restaurant, Tanner is already seated at a high-top table, a beer in his hand, and there is one waiting for me.

"Hey." We do the handshake/hug thing, and then I sit across from him and sip the beer. "What's the occasion?"

"Sarah, Luna, and June are at the chapel. June wants opinions on something or other. Wolfe should be here soon."

"Cool. How are things at the gallery?"

Tanner owns Whalers Gallery, an art studio in town. He's always been interested in art, even when we were kids, so when he studied art in college, it wasn't a surprise. Whalers Gallery is a fantastic place, and a popular one for the tourists.

"They're great. The summer season was *really* good. I can report that tourism is alive and well in Huckleberry Bay."

"Excellent." We clink beers just as Wolfe walks over and takes a seat.

"No beer for me?"

"You said you may be awhile, and I didn't want it to get warm," Tanner replies.

"Yeah, we were working on a bitch of a transmission." Wolfe blows out a breath and waves to the bartender, who waves back, already knowing Wolfe's order. "I left it to Zeke and got the hell out of there," he continues.

"That's what business partners are for," I reply with a grin. "I think I'm about to take on a partner and a few employees. I can't keep up with my workload alone anymore."

"You haven't looked great," Tanner says, and I glare

at him. He holds up his hands as if in surrender. "I'm sorry, I don't mean that to sound like a jerk, but you've

been working too damn much, and it shows. You look tired and grouchy as fuck."

I'm tired because I work too hard.

I'm grouchy because June won't give me the time of the goddamn day, and I crave her in a way I've never craved anything or anyone before.

That absolutely is *not* something I'm going to admit to anyone, not even my two best friends.

"It was a busy-as-hell summer," is all I say, and the other two nod in understanding. All three of us own businesses in Huckleberry Bay. Wolfe has the garage, which is newly rebuilt and equipped to fix anything that a vehicle could need repaired. He also owns a sweet-as-fuck personal garage where he works on and restores muscle cars.

That place is a gearhead's wet dream.

"But I won't complain about having work because, for a while there, new construction was hard to find. So, I'll hire more people and pick and choose the projects I want to personally take on."

"Good call." Tanner nods and then smiles when the bartender and owner of Lighthouse Pizza comes to the table with Wolfe's beer.

"You fellas ready to order?" Harvey asks after slapping me on the back. "You want your usual large pie?"

"And another large to go," Wolfe adds. "I'll take one to the girls on my way home."

"I know how they like it." Harvey winks before walking back to the bar to put in the order.

"I met with June at the chapel today," I inform the other two. "She's starting the renovations and wants to be living there by the holidays."

"That's fast," Wolfe says with a frown. "She'll work herself to death."

"Isn't that the same amount of time it took to build your entire, enormous barndominium?" Tanner reminds him.

"Yeah, but I used a big company out of Portland. June plans to do most of it herself. She'll hire out the electrical and plumbing, but it's still going to be a lot of work."

"I'll make sure it happens," I mutter, staring into my beer. "If that's what she wants, she'll damn well have it."

Harvey delivers the pizza, and I pull a slice onto my plate. When I go to take a bite, I realize the other two are staring at me, ignoring the pizza altogether.

"What?"

"You're totally gone over June," Tanner says.

"Yeah, I'm into the woman who can't stand the sight of me, insults me every chance she gets, and only barely tolerates me because she's best friends with my little sister."

"You *are* a masochist, man," Wolfe replies with a grin. "But, hey, we're not here to judge."

"June's important to Luna, so if she wants her house done, we'll do it. She busted her ass for the inn, so it's the least I can do."

"Uh-huh." Tanner grins, finally pulling a piece of pizza onto his plate. "Right. You're *repaying* her."

"Shut the fuck up."

"You know," Wolfe says around a bite of food as Tanner chuckles with hilarity, "it's always amazed me that despite the chippy banter between the two of you, there's also a shit ton of chemistry. Just fuck her already."

Been there, done that, and would do it again if she'd let me.

"As much as I appreciate this little trip into my personal life and nonexistent lovesickness for June, can we change the subject now? You two have better things to do than write fairy tales about me."

"Do you even know why she doesn't like you?" Tanner asks, semi-seriously.

"Nope." I sip my beer, thinking about it. "But she's been like this since she was a kid—probably middle school. I always ignored her back then, but now we all hang out together a lot, and she's hard to ignore."

"She's pretty," Wolfe says. "Yeah, she has the tomboy thing down with the coveralls and hats, but even that can be sexy."

"She's always had the prettiest red hair," Tanner agrees, and all I do is narrow my eyes at the two of them.

"What are you trying to do?"

"Nothing." Wolfe polishes off his slice and reaches for another. "Just pointing out that June's hot. It's fine if you're not into her. Someone will snatch her up."

"She's a catch." Tanner nods, looking into his glass.

"Don't be stupid." I sit back and wipe my hands on a

napkin. "Do you live in the sixties? Women don't need to be 'snatched up'. She's fine and does damn well without any help from anyone else."

I shake my head, surprised that they're talking about *any* woman this way.

"You two idiots are better than that. Luna and Sarah don't *need* you. Either of you."

"You're absolutely right."

Tanner is grinning. They both are.

"You two are assholes."

They laugh and fist-bump, and I sigh.

"You sure didn't like the idea of her being with someone else."

"I think you ought to mind your own damn business."

We finish dinner, and Harvey passes Wolfe a fresh pizza on our way out.

"You guys coming with me?" Wolfe asks.

"I'll go over," Tanner says with a nod.

"I'm out." I shake my head and start for my truck. "I have another early morning tomorrow. Have a good night."

"See ya," Wolfe calls out.

Do I want to see June? Hell yes. I want more than that. But I already spent time with her today, and it was all my system could handle.

It's almost torture to be so close to her and know that I can't touch her or kiss her.

That night we spent together was a fucking mistake because now I'm addicted to her, and I can't have her.

It's fucking horrible.

"Well, what are you doing here so early?"

Luna smiles at me, holding a steaming mug of coffee as she sits inside the gazebo by the lighthouse and watches the sky come to life over the Pacific Ocean.

"I thought I'd swing by on my way to a job and see how things are going here," I say, sitting next to her on the bench.

"They're so good. The inn is 99 percent finished, and we're ready to bring in furniture. I get to stage everything and make it extra pretty."

"It's hard to believe that it's almost finally done."

"Oh, I can believe it. It feels like we've been working on it forever. A lot has happened in the past year from Wolfe coming home, to the fire, and Sarah being hurt by her psycho ex, and on top of it, we had to rebuild Wolfe's garage *and* continue to build the inn."

"Busy year," I agree and take a sip of coffee from the travel mug I brought with me. "This place doesn't look the same as it did when we were kids."

"Does that bother you?" She turns in her seat to face me, concern written all over her face. She's always been the pleaser in the family. "This property is your home as much as it's mine."

"I don't think that's necessarily true." I shake my head and look out at the water. "Sure, we both grew up here, but the lighthouse is in your blood, Luna. This is your home and your legacy for your new family. I like to come up to hang out, and I have good memories here, but

25

it's not my home. If you need my approval on everything that you've accomplished, you have that. I'm damn proud of you. I know Mom and Dad are, too, and they're excited to come for the holiday parties and stuff you have planned."

"I'm excited for that, too," she murmurs. "I just didn't want you to think that I took over and changed this place without having you in mind."

"You've checked in with me several times in the past year, and I have always said the same thing—do whatever you want. I mean that. You aren't foolish, you love this property, and you're going to make it really awesome."

"Okay. That makes me feel better. What are you up to today?"

"I have a job up in Lincoln City."

"That's quite a ways away."

I nod and sip my coffee. "Yeah, that's why I'm getting an early start. I'll finish it up today, and then I'm back in Huckleberry Bay for the foreseeable future. What about you?"

"The cleaning crew finished yesterday, so I'm going to start going through the deliveries of décor and stuff for the inn that I've gotten over the last couple of weeks."

"So, you really are ready to go."

"I am." She does a little shimmy in the seat. "It'll probably take most of the day, and Sarah and June care coming to help. We also get to hang all the artwork that Sarah did for the guest rooms."

"That'll be awesome. I'll come by when I'm done with work and see if I can lend a hand."

"I'll take all the help I can get. Then, June needs to get opinions on some outfits from Sarah and I later, so she's bringing those with her."

I scowl. "Outfits? That doesn't sound like June."

"Oh, you don't know her. She always has to get our opinions when she has to wear girl clothes for something."

"What's the occasion?"

"She's going on a date."

I almost choke on my coffee, and Luna hurries to pat me on the back. "Easy, don't inhale that."

"I'm okay." I clear my throat. "June has a date, huh?"

"Yeah, with some guy who recently moved to town. I forget his name. Anyway, they met at the coffee shop a few days ago, and he asked her out. I was kind of surprised she agreed since June's never been super interested in dating, but I'm excited for her."

I have no right to be this fucking pissed off.

We've never made promises to each other—hell, she can't fucking *stand* me, but I want to shake some sense into her and punch the other guy out.

"I think he's taking her to dinner at Three Sisters," Luna continues. "That'll be nice."

"Hmm. I'd better get to it."

"Oh, sorry to hang you up. I'm babbling." She grins and stands with me before giving me a big hug. "Thanks for being such an awesome brother."

"I'm only mediocre, at best."

"Nope, you're awesome. You could have been a big jerk about this whole inn thing."

27

"Only an asshole would do that. I should be done in Lincoln City by noon, and then I'll be by to see what I can help with."

"Awesome. I'll save the hard-to-reach stuff for you."

I laugh and wave as I get into my truck, and then I drive down Lighthouse way and turn toward the highway.

June has a goddamn date. And it isn't with me.

"WHERE DO THESE PILLOWS GO?"

I walk into pandemonium.

There are pillows, blankets, lamps, and cushions all over the foyer. On the steps, there are rolled-up rugs, and there are even more blankets hung over the newel post.

It looks like Pottery Barn threw up in here.

"In the library!" is the answer shouted upstairs.

"Uh, hello?" I walk back to the kitchen and find all three Kinnard sisters hard at work, storing dishes and cutlery, pots and pans, and more dry goods than I could count.

"Hi, Apollo," Cordelia says with a happy smile. She blows a strand of hair out of her eyes. "It's move-in day."

"I heard. I came to see if I can help. Have you seen my sister?"

"I think I heard her upstairs," Mira says, shaking a big-ass knife in that general direction. "I made some lemon tarts and fresh sweet tea for everyone to snack on. This is hard work."

"I'll definitely be back for that." I wink at her and then set off in search of Luna so I can get my marching orders.

But when I get to the top of the stairs, I'm met with a *very* fine ass.

June—I'd recognize that ass anywhere—is bent over, storing perfectly folded sheet sets in a cupboard.

"I swear to god," she mutters, "this is a pain in the ass. Why didn't she have me build her a whole linen closet? No, she had to have an antique cupboard that's *aesthetically pleasing*."

I can't help but smile. I love it when Juniper talks to herself.

"Need some help?"

She jumps in surprise and hits her head on the shelf. As she rubs the sore spot, she turns to glare at me.

"From you? Hell no. Why are you lurking behind me? Are you staring at my ass? You're a perv."

"It's a nice ass." I shrug, as if I'm not at all bothered by her rudeness. The truth is that I'm *not*. I love the sass that comes out of this woman.

It fucking turns me on.

"Luna's in one of the guest rooms that way." She points down the hall before turning back to putting the sheets into the cabinet, but I don't walk away. "Leave me alone, Apollo."

"Nah. I don't think I will." I get closer, grab one of the sheet sets that needs to be stored, and smooth out the fabric. "I think that, if you fold these one more time, they'll fit better."

"I didn't ask you." She yanks the set out of my hands and works her damn hardest to ignore me.

She smells amazing, and being so close to her, I can feel the warmth coming off her. I remember how warm her skin is, how responsive.

She's pulled her riot of red curls into a twisted knot, which is a feat in and of itself. Her hair is thick and long, and she loves it when I bury my fist in it at her nape and give it a tug.

"You're still here."

I clear my throat. "You're observant."

"You're not good at rejection." She spins and, just like Cordelia did downstairs, blows a stray strand of hair out of her eyes. But *unlike* when Cordelia did it, it makes me want to touch her.

Before I can stop myself, I reach out and tuck the strand behind her ear. She doesn't flinch away from my touch, but her eyes narrow.

"I didn't say you could touch me."

"You're so...*bitchy*, Juniper."

Her eyes widen and, if I'm not mistaken, fill with hurt.

"I am not."

"Yeah, you are. I'm not saying that I don't like it, but damn, cut a guy a break. I don't mean any harm."

I step away from her entirely and shake my head. She has made it plain as day that she wants nothing to do with me, and yet here I am, like a lovesick puppy, trying to make moves on her.

Trying to be *nice* to her.

It's a lost fucking cause.

"I'll go find Luna."

I turn to walk away, but June grabs my arm. "Apollo."

I stop and raise an eyebrow as I look back at her. "Yeah?"

"I don't mean to be bitchy."

"Right." I nod, look down at her hand, and then back up at her. The guys are right, she's beautiful. In every way.

She also wants literally less than nothing to do with me. Hell, she's going out with someone else *tonight*.

It doesn't get any clearer than that.

"Don't worry, Juniper, I'll leave you be. Luna's that way?"

Her mouth opens, but then she sighs. "Yeah. That way."

"Thanks."

I walk down the hall and hear Luna laughing with Sarah. When I get to the doorway, I can't help but grin. They're making the bed, but they're in stitches over something, laughing so hard that they're crying.

Sarah slowly slides to the floor as if she has no more muscle strength, which has Luna laughing harder.

"What's so funny?"

"Oh, my god, so funny," Luna manages to get out and then wipes at her eyes before waving away my question. "But it would get lost in translation. You made it."

"I did. What do you need me for?"

"So many things. I have some tables and chairs that need to be brought into the dining room, and if you could bring the rugs that are on the stairs up here, I would appreciate it."

"Is there any more man power on the way?"

"Wolfe should be here soon, and if we're still here working when Tanner closes the studio, he'll come by. At this rate, we'll be here all night."

"Are the tables and chairs assembled?" I ask her.

"Yes. And they're also heavy since I got really nice pieces that will last a long time, but we can help you."

"I'll go down and start with the chairs," I reply. "Wolfe and I can move the tables later."

"There are rugs already in the dining room and unrolled so they would relax. You should be good to go in there."

"Perfect." I offer her a mock salute and then head back for the stairs, not a little relieved when I see that June has already moved on to another task.

It's time I get June out of my system and move on.

Chapter Three

June

"I don't know what I was thinking. I'm *not* wearing this," I hiss into the phone as I stare at the mirror in horror. "What were *you* thinking?"

"That top looks *stunning* on you," Luna assures me.

"But I'm showing cleavage, and this bra is ridiculously uncomfortable. I'm too big to wear something that boosts me up like this. I look like I should be working at Hooters or something."

"Good, that means you look hot, but if you're uncomfortable, wear something else. That's the most important thing, *comfort*."

"No, I'm trying new things, for God's sake. I'm thinking outside the box, and I freaking hate it."

"I can assure you that, if you're wearing what we decided on at the inn this afternoon, you look great. We wouldn't tell you to wear something horrible. You don't look slutty, and you aren't really showing that much cleavage, just more than you're used to."

"Feels like a lot," I mutter and turn to the side to get a look at my ass. "These jeans are really tight on my ass, too."

"You have a great ass."

The same words from Apollo echo in my mind. Seeing him today, having him so close to me, has really knocked me off my game. Now I'm second-guessing myself, *and* I feel guilty for going on a date when I have nothing to feel guilty about.

"June, do you want my advice?"

"That's why I called you."

"Wear the outfit. Feel confident in it. You're sexy, and even if this first date doesn't turn into a second date, you're still sexy. You've got this."

"Yeah." My hair is down, and the curls are tamed. I'm wearing makeup for the first time in more than a year, and thanks to Sarah and June, it actually looks pretty good.

I look like a girl.

"Okay, I'm meeting him at Three Sisters because I refused to let him pick me up at my grandma's house and get the third degree from her. Plus, if he's horrible, I can just leave."

"Good plan. I like it. Stay safe, and call me if you need me."

"Okay. I'll call you tomorrow. Thanks."

I hang up, frown at myself in the mirror, and then throw my hands up before hurrying to pull on the one and only pair of black dress shoes I own. They're going to kill my feet, but at least they match my top and they aren't heels.

I draw the line at heels.

After tossing my phone, wallet, and lip gloss into the tiny bag that Sarah loaned me, I walk out of the room I've lived in since I discovered mold in my rental last year and had to move out, and hurry down the stairs to find Grandma sitting in the living room watching *Jeopardy*.

"I'm headed out for the evening."

"Be safe out there," she says before looking over, but after a second, she turns to me, and her eyes just about bulge out of her skull. "Well, look at you."

"It's just an outfit."

"No, that's an *outfit*. You must have a date."

"Yeah. I decided to look like a girl for it."

"You're so beautiful," she says as her eyes fill with tears.

"Don't cry."

"I'm almost eighty years old. Don't you tell me what to do." She sniffles but then smiles. "Have a wonderful time, my dear."

"I'll try." I lean over, kiss the top of her head, and then I'm off.

My truck could practically drive itself the short distance into the heart of downtown Huckleberry Bay, it's made the trip so many times. When I pull into the parking lot of Three Sisters Kitchen, it isn't too packed for a Friday night, and I easily find a spot.

"What am I doing?" I whisper, not ready to get out of the truck yet. I'm not good at dating, and they usually end up in disaster. Am I trying to wash Apollo out of my brain?

Maybe.

"Don't be dumb. It's one evening, and Eric seemed nice. Just go inside already."

It wasn't my best pep talk, but it does the trick because I unhook the seatbelt, step out of the truck, and lock the doors before walking inside.

"Well, hello, hottie." Darla looks me up and down and then fans her face. With her being the third sister and part owner of Luna's new inn, I've grown to know Darla well over the past year. She's funny and hardworking. I really like her.

"Don't make me punch you."

Darla laughs. "You really *do* look great. I take it you're meeting Mr. Eric? He said he was meeting a date here."

I love the way all three Kinnard sisters have that soft southern drawl hanging in their voices. They moved here about six years ago from South Carolina, I think, and listening to them talk is always so soothing.

"I'm the date."

"I'll show you the way."

I take a deep breath and then follow Darla through the dimly lit, busy restaurant to a table in the back where Eric's waiting for me.

I met him at The Grind a few days ago, and he struck up a conversation with me while we waited for our coffee. The conversation was easy and fun, so when he asked me out, I accepted without really giving it much thought.

I'm glad I did. He's tall, with dark blond hair, green eyes, and broad shoulders. His smile might be *too* perfect.

Honestly, now that I think about it, he looks like a Ken doll with scruff.

"Wow." Eric stands and leans in to kiss my cheek. "You look fantastic."

"Thanks." This might be the most compliments on my looks that I've ever received in my life. Do I really look that bad on a daily basis? Because it's getting almost insulting.

"What can I get you to drink, June?" Darla asks as I sit.

"Just water for me tonight, thanks."

"Sure thing." She fills my glass from a pitcher and then leaves me alone with Eric to peruse the menu. I haven't been this nervous in a *long* time. "Have you been here before?"

"No, but I like the atmosphere. How about you?"

"Yeah." I nod slowly and glance over the familiar menu before I set it aside, knowing what I'll order. "I know you're new to town, but you didn't mention where you moved from. How long have you been here?"

"New York City, actually, but I'm not quite here full time yet." The way he says that makes it seem like I should be impressed.

I'm not.

"This is very different from New York. What brought you here?"

"Work. I'll admit that I'm not a small-town guy. I already miss the city."

"I find it hard to believe that there are more job opportunities in Huckleberry Bay than in New York City."

He smiles as if I just said the most adorable thing ever. I don't like it. I can already see that this *won't* turn into a second date.

"Of course not, but I've decided to open a boutique hotel here in town, and I've been scouting different locations to build."

I nod slowly, taking that in. "I've heard some rumblings about that. Have you decided on a piece of property?"

"I think so. There's a lot off Main Street that would be big enough for my needs."

Alarm bells go off in my head as I realize that he might be talking about the lot next to my chapel. That's the only empty lot in town, and I do *not* want a big hotel next to my house.

"Is there a church nearby?"

"Yeah, that's the one." He smiles, trying so hard to be charming. "I'll buy the church, as well, and knock that down. The whole area is an eyesore. The hotel will be a big improvement for the town."

"You think so?" I tilt my head, trying not to show my annoyance. I've never had a great poker face, but I don't want him to see just how irritated I am. Not yet. "We already have a new inn up at the lighthouse, you know."

"I know. I'll have them out of business within a year."

Okay, I really don't like Eric at all. "Besides, a successful hotel like mine will be a magnet for all kinds of businesses."

"We have all kinds of businesses already."

"I'm talking about making Huckleberry Bay a functioning town."

I clear my throat, and when Darla comes over to take our order, I smile up at her, choking down the curse words I want to spew at the jerk across from me. "I need a few more minutes, please."

"No worries." She tops off my water glass and then bustles away.

"Are you implying that Huckleberry Bay isn't a functioning town *now*?"

Here comes that condescending smile again. "June, it's a tiny town. It's like a baby. It needs a little nurturing, a little help."

"For what goal? What do you envision this town to look like as an adult?"

"Okay, we can do this." Eric leans back in his chair. "I think it needs to double, maybe triple, in size. Cater more to the tourists, and offer more in the way of vacation homes that are bigger and more updated than what is currently available. There needs to be theater, art, and better restaurants. This one is good, but the town needs more places to dine, possibly some of the national chains, as well as more hotels."

He says the town needs more hotels, yet his one-year goal is to put Luna out of business. That makes zero sense.

"And where would we put these things? We're a seaside town, Eric."

"There's plenty of space for growth, sweetie."

"Says who?" I make a point of ignoring the disgusting term of endearment.

He tilts his head to the side, watching me. "You don't think those things would be valuable here?"

"No, I don't."

"I guess it's true what they say—if you've never had it, you don't miss it. You must not be very well traveled."

I'm not irritated anymore. I'm pissed. "I've traveled plenty. I *like* the town the way it is, and so do most of the people who live here. I can't believe the city officials would ever agree to all of this expansion."

"They haven't yet. It's all part of the long-term vision I have, and why I want to build the hotel. I should close on the property in the next thirty days, sixty at the most, and break ground in the spring. I'm here to make sure that everything is lined up and ready to go, and then I'll go back to New York until we begin the build. God knows I don't want to spend the winter in this hellhole."

"No, you wouldn't want that." I give him a wide, toothy smile, holding myself back from reaching out to smack him. "I guess I'm curious as to why you asked me out tonight. I'm certainly not your type, and you're only here for a short time."

"True," he immediately replies, and it's so idiotic that it doesn't even hurt my feelings. "I thought you were funny, and you intrigued me. My instincts were right, too, because you clean up very well."

I want to punch him. Not just smack him.

"Sure, I'm only here for a few days, but we can have a lot of fun in those few days." He winks at me over his glass, but then his eyes drop to my cleavage before returning to my face.

"Right. You know, I think I'm going to pass on dinner."

"Okay." He blinks in surprise, and then he tosses a couple of twenties onto the table to cover his drink and tip and follows me out of the restaurant. "Good idea. We can cozy up at my rental and get to know each other better."

I'm not going to make a scene in this restaurant and embarrass my friends, so I wait until we reach the driver's side of my truck, and I turn to him.

"No, I'm not saying that I want to skip dinner so we can have sex. I'm saying I'm not interested in *anything* with you, Eric. This date was a mistake."

His handsome face twists into an angry snarl.

"What are you, some kind of fucking tease?"

"No, I'm an intelligent woman who knows an arrogant, narcissistic asshole when she sees one. You can go back to New York, Eric."

I turn to open the door, but he yanks on my shoulder, pulling me back around to face him.

"Listen, you bitch—"

"No, *you* listen. Take your hands off me. I didn't give you permission to touch me."

"You small-town, white-trash hillbilly, I'll fucking *touch* you all I want."

41

He grabs for my face, to cup it in a twisted charade of a sweet kiss, and I pull back and punch him in the stomach as hard as I can.

He doubles over in pain, the wind knocked right out of him.

I lean over him. "I said don't fucking touch me."

"Gonna," he wheezes in a breath, "sue you."

Now *that* makes me laugh. "You go right ahead, *sweetie.*"

Eric straightens, and the anger shooting from his eyes tells me that I might be in for a fight—a *physical* fight, which is fine by me.

"Go ahead," I urge. "You want to put your hands where they don't belong again, Eric? Go ahead, and see what that gets you."

He looks like he wants to tear me apart, but instead, he throws out, "Fuck you, bitch," before stomping off to his rental car and peeling out of the parking lot.

I let out a long breath, shake my head, and turn to my truck, freezing when I see Apollo standing on the other side of it. His jaw is tight, every muscle in his face set in angry lines, and his body looks like he was poised and ready to come save me from that asshole.

Then he relaxes and just watches me with those dark eyes.

Shit.

"Were you going to save the damsel in distress?"

"I don't see one of those." He looks around and then back at me. Anger still hovers in his eyes. "You handled yourself very well."

"No city boy is ever going to get one over on me. What a prick."

"Yeah. He's a prick. You okay?"

"Mostly, I'm pissed off. He didn't hurt me physically. Jesus, I didn't even have time to order a drink before he pissed me off so badly that I got up and left. He thought that was an invitation to come with me."

"Sounds like he's an idiot."

"Yeah." I blow out a deep sigh. "I guess I'll go home and wash off this war paint."

Apollo frowns. "Seems like a waste to me. Why don't you and I go inside and have dinner? I'm starving, and you have to have worked up an appetite with that right jab to the gut."

My lips twitch. "Yeah, I guess I did. I *was* looking forward to Mira's meatloaf."

"And I'd say you've earned it. Come on, Juniper, let's eat."

I walk around the truck, and when Apollo holds his hand out for mine, I eye it warily.

"Truce, for tonight. No funny stuff," he says, still holding out his hand.

"Truce." I take it, and he gives mine a little reassuring squeeze. "I can do that."

When we walk inside, Darla looks a little startled and then worried. "June, are you okay? I saw you hurry out, but—"

"I'm great," I say, offering her a reassuring smile. "We'd like a table for two, please. Not the same one from before."

"You got it." She winks at me and leads us to a table on the opposite wall. "Just water?"

"No, I want a dirty martini with three blue-cheese-stuffed olives, please."

Darla laughs. "You got it, babe. How about you, Apollo?"

"I think I'll be the one to stick with water for now."

When she leaves, I take a long, deep breath, not missing the way Apollo's eyes skim over my outfit and hair.

"If you tell me that I clean up nicely, I'll punch *you* in the stomach."

That makes him smile. "You look pretty tonight, but you were no less pretty this afternoon."

That takes me off guard, so I frown and glance out the window to the darkness beyond. I know that there's a view of the ocean here, but it's too dark to see it.

"What did he say?" I glance his way again, and he keeps talking. "To make you get up and leave?"

"Well, aside from being a jerk in general, I didn't like the way he spoke about Huckleberry Bay."

That makes Apollo's eyebrows climb in surprise, so I settle in and tell him about what Eric had to say, pausing only to place my order for meatloaf with Darla.

"What an asshole. Who is he that he thinks he can come in here and change the town?" he asks.

"Apparently, he thinks he's come kind of mogul." I shrug, wishing I'd punched the asshole in the face instead of the stomach. "But the worst part is that he says he's going to put Luna out of business."

"Absolutely not." Apollo shakes his head.

"I don't want him to buy the property next to my chapel," I reply, thinking it over. "If it's the lot I think it is, which I'm pretty sure it is, the same people I bought the chapel from own it. I'll go talk to them."

"Has he made an offer yet?"

"It didn't sound like it, and I didn't think it was even for sale."

"Let me know if you need help with that." He sighs and sips his water. "Okay, let's not talk about the asshole anymore—unless, of course, you're still upset and need to continue to vent. Then, I'm all ears."

"I'm fine." I wave him off and unwrap my silverware from the green cloth napkin. "He was a jerk. I'm over it, and I still get this amazing meatloaf. How was your day?"

"It was busy," he says with a smile that I swear to Christ lights up the whole room. Apollo smiles at me all the time, but usually, it's because he's trying to needle his way under my skin. He hardly ever genuinely smiles at me. Well, except for that one night, which I absolutely shouldn't be thinking about right now. I like it more than I should. "I had a job up in Lincoln City this morning, and then I helped out Luna until just an hour or two ago."

"And then you came here for dinner?"

He pauses and then shakes his head. "No. I was driving by on my way home, and I saw you storm out the door toward your truck with that asshole hot on your heels. I wanted to make sure you were okay."

"It's always good to know that I have backup in case I

need it." I chuckle, but he doesn't laugh with me. His lips twitch, but he's watching me so intently that it makes me want to squirm in my seat. I refuse to do that. "I appreciate it, and for the record, I'm not bitchy."

He raises his eyebrows again in surprise. "You're not?"

"I don't mean to be." I do squirm in my seat this time and hate myself for it. "You just irritate the hell out of me, and when I talk to you, I end up sounding like a complete ass, but it's your fault."

Now he *does* laugh. "It's *my* fault that you're in a bad mood every time I'm around you?"

"Absolutely. Yes."

"Why?"

I take a bite of meatloaf, thinking it over. "Damn, this is *so good*."

"Don't do that."

My eyes fly to his. "Do what?"

"Moan like that." He shifts in his seat and frowns, as if he's uncomfortable. His jaw clenches. "Answer the question."

"Because you're too much," I say and take another bite. "You're too handsome, you're too nice, and you're too *Apollo*."

"Those things irritate you?"

"Drive me up the damn wall," I agree.

"Well, you drive me nuts, too, so maybe we're even."

"And how do I do that if I'm, as you put it, always *bitchy*?"

"Exactly." He points the business end of his fork at

me and then takes a bite of his potatoes. "You're sassy, moody, a good friend, and you can be the sexiest thing I've ever seen when you're in your dirty coveralls and trucker hat with your hair all messy. Then you turn around and look like this"—he gestures vaguely my way with that fork—"and you're just as hot."

"So, I'm bitchy *and* hot, and that irritates you?"

"Hell yes."

We've stopped eating and are just staring at each other.

"We're weird people, Apollo."

"Don't I know it," he mutters and then digs into his steak. "But I can't help it. We might be really good together, you know."

"We can't date each other." I shake my head and reach for my martini, realize my glass is empty, and wave down Darla. "I need another one, please."

"You betcha," she says with a wave.

"We can't date each other," I say again, "because we'd end up killing each other, Apollo. I don't want to die young."

His lips twitch into that sexy-as-hell smirk that he always flings my way. "But what a way to go, Juniper."

"Yeah, there's that." I nibble on my lip. "What if we tried to get each other out of our systems for a while?"

"You mean, we hang out?" He's toying with me, and damn if I don't like it. "Binge-watch some TV, maybe have a healthy cooking competition?"

"That"—I nod slowly—"and, I mean, we could...you

know. Be naked together. If we decided that sounded fun."

"I did enjoy the naked part."

I stop talking as Darla sets my new drink down and takes the old glass away, but my gaze never leaves Apollo's.

"I don't want to tell the others."

"What do you mean?"

I take a sip of my new martini. "I don't want to tell Luna and the others that we're having a little fling. I don't want the questions or any of the attention. It's just you and me and nobody else."

"So, you want us to be a secret?" I can tell by the way his eyes narrow that he doesn't like that idea.

"No, I don't want to tell the others because we're only enjoying each other." I frown. "It isn't keeping it a secret so much as not sharing it with them."

"We live in a small town, Juniper. They probably already know that you're having dinner with me tonight in *public*. There are no secrets in this town."

"It's not a secret," I insist. "It's just...not anyone else's business. That's all."

"I'm not crazy about that part, but the rest of it sounds damn good to me."

"Great, no-strings sex."

"Whoa." He holds up his hands and shakes his head. "That's not what I'm agreeing to. I plan to *date* you, Juniper, to see you on a regular basis outside of the little friend group we have going on. Yes, I also plan to have a lot of sex and enjoy you, but it's not only about the sex. If that's what you want, I'm not the right guy for that job."

I'm back to chewing on my lip, wondering if I misheard him. So, he doesn't just want to fuck? He wants to, like, have a relationship?

Who even am I right now that I'm considering this?

"Okay, but we still don't say anything to the others for a little while."

"For a little while is fine."

I nod and offer him my hand. "Should we shake on it?"

He takes it, but instead of shaking it, he lifts my knuckles to his lips, kissing them softly, and I feel it all the way up my arm, down my torso, and all the way to my lady parts.

Holy hot damn.

December 5, 2019

Dear Diary,

How is it even possible that we had a freak snowstorm so early in the year? It's not even technically winter yet, and all the old-timers in town are saying that this has never happened before. We got twelve inches overnight! It's been a HUGE pain in my ass, too. Some of my projects weren't prepped properly, and we lost some lumber, which isn't going to be cheap to replace.

The worst part, though, was that my truck got stuck in Grandma's driveway, and Apollo freaking Winchester had to come help me pull it out because all the tow trucks were so busy this morning. I wanted to kiss that smug grin right off his hot face, and that only made me more irritated. Why is he so hot? And why do I have to see him so freaking often?

I'm exhausted from a horrible day, so I'll sign off now. Let's hope the snow melts PRONTO!

Xo,

June

Chapter Four

Apollo

I want her *now*. Hell, I'd clear this table and take her on top of it in front of everyone in this restaurant if I thought she'd let me.

But that asshole did some damage earlier, even if she won't admit it, so I'll take it slow tonight. It's no hardship for me since I enjoy listening to her talk, watching all the emotions play over her expressive, gorgeous face.

When I saw her storm out of Three Sisters earlier, I about swallowed my tongue. I don't remember the last time I saw June dressed up like this. Usually, dressing up means clean jeans, a sweater, and her hair brushed into a tidy ponytail.

This is next level, and while it's fun and different, I wasn't lying when I said that she isn't any less beautiful on a daily basis.

Jesus, she could wear a burlap sack, and I'd still want her.

Then, when I saw that jerk yelling at her, I wanted to

pound his face in.

June can handle herself, so no matter how badly I wanted to step in, I didn't let myself. I stood by, just in case she needed a hand.

She didn't.

"What are you daydreaming about?"

I blink and shake my head. "Sorry. Nothing important."

"You must be tired after your long day." She pushes her empty plate away and sighs happily. "That was delicious."

"Should we share dessert?"

She scoffs, and I'll be damned if that scowl doesn't make my dick twitch. "Get your own dessert, dude. I want the mud pie all to myself."

"Selfish." I click my tongue, but when Darla comes back to the table, I smile up at her. "June will have your mud pie. I think I'll try the key lime pie, and I'll have coffee."

"Me, too, please," June chimes in.

"Both excellent choices. I'll have those right out."

"Thanks."

Darla takes our dishes, and when she moves back to the kitchen, there is a spring in every step.

"You know, as the owner, Darla doesn't *have* to wait tables."

"She likes it," June replies with a shrug. "She enjoys being with the customers, and she's also really good at placating the jerks. It's her gift."

"She's great at it." I watch June for a moment and

then I can't help but say, "You know, I like having a truce with you. Sparring back and forth is exhausting."

"Yeah, well, I'm bitchy, so it'll still happen from time to time, I'm sure."

I blow out a breath. "Listen, I didn't say that to hurt your feelings."

She barks out a laugh and flips that amazing red hair over one shoulder. "Really? Did you think I'd be flattered? If that's the case, your charm needs some work, Romeo."

"I think I was being brutally honest. Frankly, your sass is sexy, but there are moments when it gets under my skin. Like when I'm trying to flirt with you or am being just plain nice to you."

"No one asked you to do those things." Her face folds into a snarl, and all I can do is chuckle at her. "And now you're laughing at me."

"Looks like our truce lasted about ninety minutes."

June sighs and then sits back as Darla places our desserts and coffees before us.

"Thanks, Darla."

"Enjoy. I think I might snag myself some key lime before it's all sold out." Darla grins before she hurries away.

"Anyway, I like to banter with you, but once in a while, I like it when you're nice to me."

"Hmm." She sips her coffee, and then she takes a bite of her mud pie, which has her eyes closing in ecstasy the same way they do when she's about to come.

It's absolutely fucking amazing.

To keep myself in check, I take a bite of my key lime and nod. "Damn good."

"Better than sex," she says almost absently before taking another bite. Then she must realize what she said because her eyes widen a bit as they find mine.

"Looks like we have some work to do if that dessert is better than what I've done to you in the bedroom."

She clears her throat, sips her coffee, and then smiles. "Yeah, you'd better step up your game, ace, because this mud pie is damn good."

"Challenge accepted."

"Of course, I didn't invite you to come home with me."

"I didn't say it would be tonight," I counter, and if I'm not mistaken, a flash of disappointment shines in those eyes, so I decide to change the subject. "How is Annabelle?"

June's grandmother has always been one of my favorite people in Huckleberry Bay. She's eclectic and funny, and while she may be getting up there in age, she'll never act like it.

"She's doing well. Getting ready for the epic Halloween party in a few weeks."

"It's my favorite party of the year." I finish my pie and then sit back to enjoy the last of my coffee. "What's the theme this year? Last year was Disney, so I'm wondering how she's going to top that."

"*The Great Gatsby*." June grins. "Grandma's in the mood to celebrate the roaring twenties. I have to buy a flapper dress."

"That'll be an experience. How is she decorating for it?"

"You know I'm not allowed to divulge all her secrets. You'll have to wait and see when you get there."

"Fine. I'll wait." June licks her fork clean, and I'm pretty sure I'm going to have an aneurysm from wanting that tongue on *me*.

When Darla brings the check, we reach for it at the same time, but I easily tug it out of June's grasp.

"You don't have to buy me dinner," she says, a small frown pinching her brow.

"I understand that I don't *have* to, but I want to. Dinner's on me." I slip my card into the folio, and Darla whisks by to take it from me. "Darla's fast."

"Now I feel guilty because you shouldn't feel like you have to buy me dinner. I should be the one to pay, since you saved me from wasting all the work I put into this outfit."

"Are you under the impression that I often do things that I don't want to do?" I ask, narrowing my eyes slightly. She should know me better than that after all these years.

"You helped out Luna today, and I'm pretty sure you would have rather been somewhere else."

"She's my sister, and if she needs a hand, I'm happy to lend it. I don't do anything that I don't want to besides pay a shit ton in taxes, and I only do that because I'm not in a hurry to see the inside of a prison cell. I wanted to buy you dinner, so I did. Thanks for coming back inside with me."

"Well, thanks for dinner," she says, but she still looks uncertain. "I guess."

"Would it make you feel better if I agreed to let you buy me coffee or lunch or something sometime?"

"Yeah, probably."

"Then you have a deal."

Her mouth opens and then closes again. Darla returns with my card, and I sign the slip.

"Why aren't you always this easygoing?" June finally asks.

"I am, remember? You're the one who's a little—"

"Bitchy."

"I was going to say uptight. I'm going to regret saying that forever, aren't I?"

"Pretty much."

I offer her my hand, but she stands without my help, and I follow her through the restaurant, waving at people we know as we pass them. Then we're pushing through the door and walking into the chill of the early autumn night air.

"I have to go to the chapel for a bit," she says softly when we reach the driver's side.

"It's after nine."

"I know, but I have to take some measurements. I've taken them before, but I want to double-check them before I place my order for lumber."

"Smart. Want some help?" I grin and rock back on my heels. "I promise that I'll keep my hands to myself."

As if to prove the point, I shove my hands into my pockets.

"Okay, you can hold one end of the measuring tape."

"At your service. I'll follow you over."

She nods and turns to get into her truck, but before she opens the door, she turns and wraps her arms around me.

"Thanks for dinner," she says. Then she abruptly lets go and climbs into her truck.

She backs out of her space and takes off toward the chapel, and I can't help but smile.

"You're welcome."

By the time I arrive at the chapel, June's already inside, and all the lights seem to be on. She didn't wait outside for me, but then again, I didn't really expect her to.

We may have a truce, but June is who she is, and I like her that way.

I jog up the steps, taking two at a time, and knock on the door before pushing it open and popping my head inside.

"You in here?"

"Yep." Her answer echoes in the mostly empty space. June's voice is rich, and it has a hint of rasp that's always been a pleasure to listen to.

That is, when she's not yelling at me.

"I have an extra tape measure in case we need it." I close the door behind me, and walk farther inside to see June squatting, a roll of blue tape in her hand. The top she's wearing is low cut, giving me an excellent view of her cleavage, but I'm smart enough not to mention it. She might injure me. "What are you doing?"

"I'm marking the space for the walls."

"Didn't you have plans drawn up for this?"

She scowls at me and blows her hair out of her eyes. "*Of course,* I have plans. I can't have anything approved through the city without them. But I want to get a better look in real life, not just on paper."

"Okay, let me help."

For about an hour, we go back and forth between the drawings and laying down long strips of blue tape so she can see where walls will be.

"This building is bigger than it looks," I say after the last piece of tape is down. "From the outside, it looks tiny, but it's spacious in here."

"Yeah, I'm wondering if I should add a small third bedroom or office in that corner at the front of the building, since I'm repurposing the old office." She points to the far end of the room and to the left of the front doors. "It would take some square footage away from the living space, but I would gain an extra room."

"Didn't you plan to use the second bedroom as your office anyway?"

"Yeah." She tugs on her lower lip, thinking it over. "But what if I have guests? I mean, I never do, but what if that changes? Adding that extra room is also great for resale value."

"Do you plan to sell?"

"Well, no, but five years from now, that might change. It's already been pointed out that this place isn't exactly a great house for kids."

That has me stopping in my tracks, and I just stare at her as all the blood leaves my face. "Are you *pregnant*?"

"Huh?" She turns to me and quickly shakes her head. "No! No, I'm definitely *not* pregnant. They just meant that if, down the road, I ever wanted to have them, this isn't a great place for that."

"Why not?" I tilt my head, wondering what exactly makes this place unacceptable for kids.

"Well, for starters, there's a cemetery in the backyard. That's not really an ideal place to put a swing set, you know?"

"There's a park one block down."

"Okay, well, there's no garage here, so that means there's not much storage space."

"You said you have an entire basement downstairs."

"An unfinished basement."

"Okay, so you finish it and use it for storage. What else?"

"Two bedrooms," she says. "Or two bedrooms and an office. It's a small place, Apollo, but it's perfect for one person or a couple—not a family."

"I'll concede that it may not be great for a growing family, but you're not pregnant right now." I look around, thinking it over. "The ceilings are really high in here. If you ever wanted to, you could add a loft or a small second floor for more bedrooms or that office space."

"Exactly. I asked them, why live off what-ifs? Why can't I live my life for today and then sell this place if I ever outgrow it?"

"I think that's the right attitude. And, besides, if you

need extra storage for your tools or whatever, I have an empty shed you could use. My place is closer, so it would save you a lot of driving back and forth."

That makes her pause, frown, and then fidget with her measuring tape.

"Okay, why did that trip you up?"

"I don't know what you're talking about. I think I'm about done here, so you can take off if you want. Thanks for your help. You made it go a lot faster than if I was by myself."

"Juniper."

"I'm going to check on something in that back room before I lock up. Thanks again for dinner."

She waves and takes off for the door, and I hurry after her, take her hand, and pull her around to face me.

"You don't need to be jumpy around me."

"Earlier I was bitchy, and now I'm jumpy. Make up your mind."

"You can swipe at me all you want, but I'm not leaving until you tell me what just set you off."

Her green eyes are blazing as she looks up at me.

"You're not the boss of me, Apollo Winchester, and if buying me dinner makes you think otherwise, I'll go fish fifty bucks out of that tiny excuse of a purse that Sarah made me carry." Her words are full of venom, but then she swallows hard and her eyes soften, as if she's sorry for what she just said.

"Why does it piss you off so much when I'm nice to you?"

"Because you're *not* nice." She plants her hands on

my chest and pushes, so I step away. "You're not nice to me, and I don't want you to be nice now, only for me to get used to it and then have you turn back into the jerk."

"Wait." I rake a hand through my hair in agitation. I want to kiss the hell out of her and shake her at the same time. "I'm not a jerk, and I think most people who know me would tell you that I *am* a decent guy."

"They don't really know you," she whispers, and I narrow my eyes on her.

"What in the world, Juniper? I don't even know *why* you don't like me. I don't understand why I'm the butt of your jokes or why you always pick little fights with me. Even when we're with our friends, you smirk, you poke, and you're just—"

"Bitchy," she finishes for me.

"Sometimes," I confirm. "Why? What did I do? Where does all of this come from?"

"You were *so* mean to me." Her voice is rising now as she starts to pace the few feet between me and the door to the future mudroom. "I was just a kid, and sure, I had a stupid preteen crush on you, but you *laughed* at me, and in front of your friends, you were like, *'Why would I be interested in a carrottop like you, kid?'*"

"I never said that to you." But, as soon as the words leave my mouth, I remember the moment she's talking about, and shame washes over me.

"Oh, you did. Yes, you absolutely did. As an adult, I can shake it off and even chalk it up to kids being kids, since most kids are pretty awful, but I was so heartbroken and so fucking *embarrassed* because you all laughed, and

61

I had enough issues about my hair at the time. It almost ruined my friendship with Luna because the thought of seeing you on a regular basis filled me with so much anxiety that I didn't think I could pull it off. But I love Luna and Sarah, and I wasn't willing to stop being friends with them, so if that meant that I had to endure time around *you*, then so be it. It didn't mean I ever had to be nice to you, though, because you didn't deserve it."

"I'm sorry, Juniper." I swallow hard, filled with shame. "I do remember that day, and we *were* horrible to you."

"Save it." She shakes her head and turns back to the door. "Let's consider the truce over, so there is no need to fuck or be nice to each other. Let's just leave it be."

"No."

I turn her to me again, ready to duck out of the way in case she takes a swing at me, but she doesn't.

Instead, I'm shocked to see that she has tears in her beautiful green eyes.

"Juniper." My voice is soft as I drag my fingers down her cheek. "Honey, I swear to you that I'm so sorry for *ever* hurting you. I was a foolish, selfish, prick of a teenager, who thought he was being cool in front of his so-called friends."

"Yeah, you were," she whispers, closing her eyes, and those tears splash onto her cheeks, effectively breaking my heart.

"If I could change it, I swear I would, but I can't. I can only apologize again. Juniper, I'm completely *obsessed* with your hair. God, it's gorgeous and feels like heaven in my hands. There isn't anything about you that I would change, and that's the God's honest truth. Look, I'm swearing it while Jesus himself watches, so you know it has to be true."

That makes a small smile tickle the edge of her lips as she glances at the stained glass window I'm pointing to.

"Those go next week, and I'm kind of glad."

"That makes two of us. Look, I want you to be comfortable around me. You have absolutely *nothing* to be embarrassed about. Hell, I'm the one who should be ashamed, and I can assure you that I am. I just wish you'd talked to me instead of holding a grudge for, what, close to twenty years?"

"Just over," she confirms.

"That's a long time."

"A really long time, but you deserved it."

"I agree. I did deserve it. Juniper, why did you have issues about your hair?"

She swallows hard and casts her eyes down, but I nudge her face up with my finger under her chin.

"My mom made fun of my hair before she left." She shrugs as if it's no big deal, but I can see in her eyes that it *is* a big deal. It makes me feel even worse for the way I treated her all those years ago. "She hated my hair. I don't know why, because the one time I asked, she just started yelling about other things. She just didn't like it. That's all."

Something tells me that isn't all there is to it, but she's told me so much more than I ever expected her to tonight, so I let it go.

Slowly, my hands drift to her shoulders as I take a small step toward her.

"I've never heard great things about your mom."

She nods, but she doesn't reply.

"Thank you for telling me what I did so I could apologize, but do you think we can move on from it? Even if we're not in a romantic relationship, I'd rather be your friend than an unwilling enemy. Besides, neither of us is going anywhere."

"I know." She blows out a breath, and her shoulders sag. "It's not easy being mad at you all the damn time."

"Then accept my apology and let me make it up to you. That way, you can hate me only when I do something really stupid."

"Which, if we're being honest, happens quite often, so I can still call you names and stuff."

"You look way too excited at that prospect."

She finally smiles, and I feel like we're through the worst of that conversation. Now that I know what she's spent so long being angry at me about, I'll probably spend a long time replaying that scene from when I was a stupid teenager in my head. "You can't teach an old dog new tricks."

"You're not old." I brush my finger down her cheek again, tracing the wet track from her tears. "Juniper, I want to kiss you so badly I ache with it."

"You can't." She swallows hard.

"Why not?"

"Because Jesus is watching."

Chapter Five

June

He licks his lips as he shifts closer to me, and my heartbeat picks up, thumping in my chest. If he aches with his want to kiss me, then we're on the same page because my skin tingles with the need for his touch.

Sometimes, we're opposing forces, and I want to push him away. Tonight, though, it's as if there is this undeniable pull that's demanding I close the small distance between us. Tonight, I want Apollo with every fiber of my being, whether Jesus is watching or not. I don't really care.

"Juniper," he whispers. My back presses against the closed door behind me. He leans his palms on either side of my head, not touching me but so damn close I can feel the heat from him and smell his soap.

I boost up onto my toes and close that gap, pressing my lips to his. He groans, and the sound of it makes my body come alive. Sliding my hands up his chest and then up higher so I can bury my fingers in that thick, dark hair, I feel like I've found heaven as he kisses me as if his life depends on it.

His hands move from the door to my ass, and he lifts me easily, pinning me in place. Instinctively, I wrap my legs around his waist and hold on as he kisses me senseless. His hands seem to be everywhere all at once, from my ass to my breasts, and then he cups my face and slows the kiss.

Not wanting to slow down *at all*, I circle my hips against him in invitation, which has him groaning once more.

"Jesus Christ, you'd tempt a fucking saint," he growls.

"Don't care about the saints." Is that *my* voice? It sounds so throaty and...needy. "Just you. Let me hop down, and I'll strip."

When he tips his forehead against mine and takes a deep breath, I know without him saying anything that we're not taking this any further tonight.

"Do I need to be embarrassed?" I ask bluntly.

"Fuck no," he replies and cups my face in his hands, looking deeply into my eyes. "I want you. I'm not playing games with you, and damn it, I'll have you again soon."

"Okay. Just making sure." I offer him a small smile, and the surprise in his dark eyes almost makes me scoff. Yeah, I can be bitchy when it comes to Apollo, but not now. "I had a surprisingly good time with you tonight."

He barks out a laugh, rests his forehead on my shoulder for a moment, and then lowers my feet to the floor.

"Same goes. I'd like to see you tomorrow."

I tilt my head, watching him. "Are we going to see each other every single day?"

"Probably not every day, but maybe every day. Does it matter?"

"No." I push my hair over my shoulder and mentally kick myself for not shoving a hair tie into my pocket before I left the house. "Just wondering if I need to pencil you into my already-booked schedule."

"I'll find you," he says with a shrug. "We'll find the time and make it work, one day at a time. So, how does tomorrow look?"

"I could do lunch," I decide. "You?"

He nods as he tucks a loose strand of my hair behind my ear. I feel the ripples from that simple touch all the way down my arm. "I can do that."

"Okay, I'll text you, and we'll figure it out."

"See how easy this is?" His smile is so disarming that it should be illegal in all fifty states.

"I can think of many words to describe you...or *us*, but easy isn't one of them."

He laughs and steps back, giving me room to breathe. "Want me to follow you home? Make sure you get there safely?"

"I've been driving myself home for a long damn time, Apollo. You don't need to follow me like you're some kind of bodyguard."

"I apologize for trying to be chivalrous." He shakes his head and walks toward the front door. "I won't do it again. By the way, this house? It's going to be fucking awesome, Juniper."

"Yeah." I bite my lower lip and look around the space, excitement growing in my belly. "It is. Thanks."

"See you tomorrow." He waves, but before he walks out, he turns to wink at me, and then he's gone.

I have to take a long, deep breath to try to calm down.

Did all of that really happen in the span of just a few hours?

"Busy night," I decide and take one more look around. I walk through the makeshift rooms, entering and exiting through the breaks in the blue tape that mark the doorways. Apollo's right. This *is* more spacious than it looks.

I lock up the chapel and then head toward my grandma's house. Only, instead of turning down the road that would take me there, I find myself turning onto Lighthouse Way and climbing the windy road to the lighthouse.

And the inn.

There are a few lights glowing inside the inn, but I know that it's empty. I'm so damn proud of the place. It started out as an old barn with rotten floors and walls, and at Luna's request, we used what we could and built the inn around the old structure. She wanted a piece of the past to remain, so that's what we gave her.

The result is absolutely gorgeous, if I do say so myself.

I park under the portico, and key in the code on the

lock to let myself in. A light shines in the foyer, and I can see another soft light glowing from the kitchen.

Luna wanted to have dim lights placed throughout the inn for nighttime, so guests would be able to navigate their way through the building after dark, without the harshness of bright bulbs.

Seeing it in the dark like this, it makes total sense.

My first stop is the small dining room. The tables and chairs are set up, complete with tablecloths and candles placed in the center of the tables. An antique sideboard sits along one wall, and will be used as a buffet for treats to sit out during the day for guests to grab and go.

I pass through to the kitchen and smile. This space is just amazing. The Kinnard sisters know their kitchens, and this one is state of the art, but it also beautifully blends into the vintage feel of the inn. Anyone would love to work back here. Mira insisted that she wanted stools to sit along the outside of the huge island so guests could come and watch her cook if they wanted to.

She may even host cooking classes here, which I think is awesome.

Maybe I'll take a class. Maybe I'll even cook for Apollo.

"Who am I right now?"

I shake my head and peek out through the glass French doors that lead to the patio I installed a couple of weeks ago. There's a view of the water in the daylight, and it's amazing.

Room by room, I make my way through and find that Luna has placed every piece of furniture, every pillow and knickknack just so. It's exactly the way she envisioned it.

Walking upstairs, I take in the rooms. Each one is themed and has a piece of original art painted by Sarah that fits in with that theme. Our sweet friend is a talented artist, and I know it meant a lot to her that Luna asked her to paint the pieces for the inn.

When I reach the last room, the largest, I'm surprised to see that the door leading out to the balcony is open.

"What in the world?" I cross over, and then I see her. Luna's sitting in one of the two outdoor chairs, a glass of wine in her hand as she watches the scene before her. "I don't want to startle you."

She turns her head and smiles at me. "Hi. I saw you drive up a few minutes ago. Figured you came to see how we did today."

"Yeah, and just to walk through, take it all in before it's full of people."

"I hear you. Sit with me." She gestures to the seat next to her and then offers me her glass. "I only have the one glass, but I'll share."

"Thanks." I take it and sip, before passing it back to her. "Wow, this view is just incredible."

"I know." She takes a deep breath, and for a long moment, we're quiet as we take in the view. The lighthouse, so tall and strong and proud, is on the left. The way the inn is situated, the lighthouse doesn't block the view of Huckleberry Bay and the ocean. "I love watching the lights from town. You can see just about everything from up here."

"Grab a pair of binoculars, and we could be regular Peeping Toms." I smile over at her. I don't know if I've ever seen Luna this serene, this *peaceful*. "You okay, friend?"

"I'm great. For the first time in over a year, I don't feel like I have to rush or worry. It's just done. I can sit up here, on this gorgeous balcony that my best friend in the whole world built for me, and I can look out over the property that I share with the man I love most in the world, and I know that I'm going to make a difference in the community that's shaped who I am. It's an incredible feeling, and for tonight, while no one else is here yet, I can just sit in the quiet and soak it in."

"Until I interrupted you."

"You're never an interruption." She smiles over at me and offers me more wine.

"Where's Wolfe tonight?"

"Still at the garage with Zeke. They got in a new car that they're geeking out over. And that's fine, because it gave me time to be here for a while. I can't wait to offer the Ford we found in the barn for rides to and from town. The guests are going to love that."

"Oh, for sure."

"Holy shit, you went on a date! How did I space on that? Tell me everything."

I take in a deep breath full of clean ocean air and let it out slowly. "Worst date of my life."

"Oh, no."

"Pretty horrible." I nod and pass back her wine. "I'll

71

wait to tell you all about it when we have Sarah with us so I only have to relive it once."

"Probably a good idea."

"But then your brother showed up, and I ended up having dinner with him." I'm not going to give her all the details. And I'm *definitely* not going to tell her that I'm going to start seeing him. Like I told Apollo, I want that just between the two of us.

But it wouldn't hurt to get her take on just this piece of it.

Out of the corner of my eye, I see her whip her head around to face me. "You did?"

"Yeah. It was nice."

"Wait." She holds up a hand and shakes her head, as if she can't believe what she's hearing. "It was *nice*? Like, you enjoyed hanging out with my brother? Apollo Winchester?"

"Yes." I want to laugh, but I just scowl over at her. "Don't make it a thing. We called a truce for the evening and had a nice meal. That's it."

"With *my* brother."

"I'm leaving." I move to stand up, but she reaches out for my arm and stops me.

"Don't go. I'm just surprised, that's all. You hate my brother."

"Hate is a strong word. I'd say he just annoys the ever loving hell out of me."

We're quiet for a minute, taking in the pretty lights of Huckleberry Bay and the sound of the surf on the cliffs below the lighthouse.

"I hope you're nicer to each other more often," she says softly. "It sucks when two of my favorite people fight all the time."

I don't answer her for a while, thinking it over. I guess I never really took into consideration how our bickering all these years has impacted Luna. Until now, she's never said anything about it.

"I'll try to be less bitchy," I say at last.

"You're not *bitchy*." Luna immediately comes to my defense, and it makes me feel so much better. "You're just stubborn."

Now, that I can't deny.

Suddenly, I smell the roses. "Rose is here."

"She's come and gone all day. I think she's been supervising as we get the place put together. You know, I had a thought today as I was making one of the beds."

"What's up?"

"Maybe Rose hangs around the property because she's not at rest. What if she's stayed here because there's something unfinished, or something that she needs?"

"I suppose that could be the case. I wish I were psychic because then I could ask her. Maybe it has something to do with Daniel, her one true love."

"Maybe." The smell of roses dissipates, and I can feel that we're alone once more. "I don't know why, but lately, I've had the feeling that she's sad. I could definitely be wrong because I'm not psychic either."

"No, but you've been with her your whole life. So if she's sad, I'm sure you can feel it."

"I wish I knew how to help her. She doesn't bother

73

me. I know she's not harmful at all, but if she should be somewhere else, I wish I could help her go there."

"One thing at a time." I reach out for her hand, and she takes mine. "You're exhausted, Luna. You worked your ass off today. I thought for sure that getting everything staged and put away would be a week-long project."

"Once I got started early this morning, I couldn't stop. I *needed* to get it all done."

"I get it. You did so great. The whole place is beautiful, and I'm sure Rose loves it, too. When do you start hosting guests?"

"Our first reservations are for Monday."

"That's less than a week away."

"Yep. The mayor and her husband will be in this room that night. We have two other rooms full, as well. I could have filled the whole place, but I thought we should start slow the first week to get our sea legs under us."

"Excellent idea."

"But then, starting next Friday, we're full every night through the holidays."

"All townspeople, on the house?"

"All townspeople," she confirms. "But most of them insisted on paying something, even if it's just to cover their food and utilities, which I thought was very sweet."

"They want you to succeed," I assure her. "Everyone is so excited and proud of you, Luna."

"I'm so glad." She pours more wine into her glass. "I'm so damn glad."

Apollo ended up having to cancel our lunch because he ran into a snafu on one of his own job sites. So, instead, I took the day to drive to a job that my crew has been on to see how things are going. While I was there, I was even able to get some paperwork done, much to the delight of my accountant, I'm sure.

The sun is just starting to set when I get to settle in at the chapel, with a fresh pile of lumber and all the supplies I need to start framing in the walls of the interior of my new house.

This has always been my favorite part of any new project, seeing it start to form before my eyes. Sure, I can see what it'll look like in my head, but watching it actually come to fruition is so satisfying.

I've just finished hammering in the last of the nails on wall number one when there's a knock at the door.

"It's open," I call out and turn to see Luna and Sarah walk in, carrying a large tote between them. "What are you guys doing?"

"We figured you'd be hungry," Sarah informs me. "So, we brought a picnic dinner, complete with an excellent wine and cake that I made myself for dessert."

"I'm so hungry." I power off the nail gun and set it aside before wiping my hands on the rag I always have hanging from the back pocket of my coveralls. "Thanks for this. You guys didn't have to go to the trouble."

"Are you kidding?" Luna asks. "We wanted to come check out the progress and have a girls' night."

"It already looks so different in here," Sarah says, looking around.

"Honestly, I'm surprised you *want* to be in here after everything that happened." I open a sandwich wrapped in parchment paper and take a bite. Flavor explodes in my mouth, and I sigh in happiness.

"The fact that it looks different helps," Sarah replies. "Also, the fact that my psycho of an ex-husband isn't in here threatening to kill me helps, too."

Neither Luna nor I laugh at that, and Sarah sighs.

"I refuse to let him have any more power over me. He took a lot of years away from me, and he doesn't get this, too. You're my bestie, and I love you. This is your home, so that's what I focus on every time I come in here. Besides, you had the floor professionally cleaned, and there's no trace of anything that happened here."

No matter how much I loved the original floors, had the cleaners not been able to remove the blood stains, I would have ripped out every board and replaced it. "The fact that you're willing to try to be as comfortable as possible is really touching and makes me feel loved."

"Good, because I *do* love you. Now, enough of that. Let's talk about how brilliant this floor plan is. Even with the blue tape lines down, I can see how well the space is going to flow."

"I agree," Luna adds before popping a potato chip into her mouth. "It's so cool. When do those windows go?"

"The crew from the church who are going to receive them was supposed to come next week, but they called today to ask if they could bring the truck on Saturday instead. I said *hell yes*. Get these windows out of here."

"Did you really say *hell yes* to the church people?" Luna asks, making me snort.

"Hell yes."

"They're pretty," Sarah says, "for a church."

"Exactly, and this is definitely no longer that. I feel really uncomfortable that Jesus is watching me a lot of the time."

They both snort laugh, and I join them.

"Okay, I have to tell you about the date from hell."

"Yes, I've been waiting all day to hear this," Luna says. "Spill it."

I do. I tell them about every second of it from the minute I arrived at Three Sisters until I found Apollo standing behind me at my truck.

"I'm so glad that Apollo was there in case that schmuck decided to try to beat you up or something," Sarah says, shaking her head. "What an asshole."

"He thinks he can drive *me* out of business?" Luna's eyes flash with anger. "As if."

"He's not going *into* business," I inform them both. "I'm meeting with Sally and Fred Newkirk tomorrow. They're the couple I bought this place from, and they own the land that Eric wants to buy. I'm going to do my best to talk them into selling to *me*."

Sarah and Luna stare at me for a second, and then they both cheer with glee.

"Hell yes," Sarah says and high-fives me. "What will you do with the property?"

"Assuming they sell it to me?" She nods. "Well, there are two buildings currently standing on it. They're abandoned, but I think I can fix them up and use them as long-term or vacation rentals. That way, it's only two rentals, not some giant hotel run by a money-hungry idiot, and they won't impact the inns and hotels in the area. No one goes out of business, and everyone is happy."

"You be careful," Luna warns me, a frown on her face. "I worry that you'll piss off this Eric guy, and he'll try to hurt you in some way."

"He can try." I shrug, not concerned in the least. "When what he wants to do to our town gets out, *no one* will sell to him. He can just tuck his tail between his legs and get his ass back to New York City."

"Still, be mindful," Luna insists.

"I won't do anything stupid. I promise."

July 4, 2012

Dear Diary,

Remind me NEVER to date someone I work with ever again, okay? That was a fucking disaster. He stole my clients and left to start his own business. What a prick. Why do all men suck so bad? Is there even one out there that isn't a complete waste of perfectly good air?

I have to go scream into my pillow now.

Xo,

June

Chapter Six

Apollo

It's been a shitty week, full of work drama that has had me running all over town from job site to job site. If I didn't know better, I'd say it was as if the universe knew that all I wanted was to spend time with Juniper, and it laughed its ass off at me.

I haven't seen her since that night in her chapel, and that's absolutely unacceptable. I crave her company, which might make me a masochist, given her fiery temperament, but it is what it is.

I want Juniper

Today, the stained glass windows are being removed from her chapel, and I wouldn't miss seeing them go for anything in the world.

When I pull up to the curb down the block, just on the far side of where the city has set up barricades so the construction crew can maneuver the crane without worrying about traffic, I realize I'm not the only one who wanted to watch the show. There's a small crowd on the sidewalk across the street. Most of them are standing around, chatting and watching the crew, but there are a handful of people who thought ahead and brought camping chairs. Smart.

I walk straight up to the chapel and go inside, surprised to see Juniper standing in the center of the space all by herself.

"Hey." I walk over to her and smile. She turns my way and quickly blinks away tears. "Whoa, what's wrong? Did something happen?"

"No." She laughs a little and wipes her eyes dry. "No, everything is fine. The crew just got here about thirty minutes ago, and they've been trying to decide the best way to take them out without damaging my walls."

"Then what made you cry?"

"It's just all finally coming together, and I'm probably hormonal or something stupid like that. It's nothing. I'm fine. What are you doing?"

"I came to watch, and I'm not the only one either. There's a little crowd gathered across the street."

"Yeah, they were standing on the sidewalk just out front, and I made them move to get out of the way. They were cool about it. It's going to be interesting to watch Jesus and the disciples flying through the air on a crane."

I nod thoughtfully. "I'm sorry I've been so busy this week."

"It's fine."

"No." With a shake of my head, I reach over, unable to keep my hands to myself any longer, and drag my finger down her cheek. "It's not fine. Let me make it up to you."

"Do I look mad?" She tilts her head to the side, and her perfect lips tip up on one side.

"Actually, no, and I know your mad face very well."

"See? Fine. It's been busy, and I get it."

There's a knock on the door. "June?"

"Yeah, Mike."

He walks in, and the way he's looking at June makes me want to punch him out.

Not that I blame him for looking at her like he'd like to eat her for lunch.

"We're ready to start. If you don't mind, we'll want the building to be empty, just in case the unthinkable happens, which it *won't*, but just in case. We have everything figured out, and there should be no damage to the structure."

"No problem." She nods and gestures for me to follow her. "Do you want us on the other side of the street with the others?"

"I don't mind if you stick close. It's your building." Mike follows us down the steps and to the side yard where the crane is parked. "They are getting ready to begin taping the windows to kingdom come to help prevent breakage. How old did you say they are?"

"About a hundred years, give or take," June replies, and Mike winces.

"Yeah, I'll have them use more tape. This is likely going to end up being an all-day job, so if you need anything from inside, I'd grab it now."

"I don't live here yet," June replies with a smile. "I'm good to go when you are, and if you need anything, let me know. I'm a professional contractor and can be put to work."

"I can, too," I offer and shake Mike's hand. "I'm Apollo. I work as an electrician, but I've done it all."

"You're both insured?"

We nod, and Mike blows out a breath. "You may come in handy, but my crew has been doing jobs like this for a long time. It's just usually not this many at once, but we'll make it happen."

"Thanks, Mike." June smiles after him, and I lean in to whisper in her ear.

"Are you trying to make me jealous?"

Her gaze whips up to mine. "What? No. Jesus."

She scowls and shoves her hands into her pockets.

"Don't be one of those men, Apollo."

"What kind would that be?"

"The kind who gets jealous over the simplest things, like a waiter in a restaurant or a guy who's removing the windows I want gone so Jesus isn't watching my every move."

"It's not my fault the guy couldn't stop checking you out—Mike, not Jesus."

"It happens." She shrugs as if it's meaningless. She's not bragging so much as stating a fact.

She's fucking adorable.

"I'm not usually jealous." I shift and cross my arms over my chest, watching as several guys walk into the chapel carrying huge rolls of tape. "I just wish you'd smile at *me* like that."

"I haven't seen you all week," she reminds me. "I haven't had the chance. But here you go."

She gives me a toothy grin, the kind that's totally fake, and I laugh.

"Happy?"

"Frankly, I want to spank your bare ass right now, but that'll have to wait."

She stammers and then closes her lips. It doesn't stop the flush from heating her pretty cheeks, and I know that it's not because she's angry.

She likes the idea.

"What? No witty response?"

"I'm thinking."

I chuckle and then look over as a police vehicle drives around the barricade and pulls up to the curb. June's brother, Cullen, gets out of the driver's seat, pulling off his aviators as he approaches us.

"It's happening," he says with some surprise.

"It's definitely happening," June agrees and rubs her hands together.

"What are you going to do about the big holes in the walls?" Cullen wants to know. "We don't have a huge homeless population, but you'll have squatters right away with gaping, empty windows."

"I'll cover them with plastic for a few days," June replies with a laugh, brushing him off. "And then, I'll have to install new framework for the new windows coming in a few days. They aren't quite as big as the original stained glass, but I want to keep the arch look since this still looks very much like an old church."

"That'll be cool," I reply. "Are you doing white or black trim?"

"Black." June grins, obviously picturing it in her head. "With the white paint, it'll look *so* cute."

"The sooner you install those new windows, the better," Cullen says. "A person can cut through plastic easily."

"Good god, Cull, what do you think's going to happen? This isn't the city. You're so cynical."

"Being a police officer tends to do that to a person because we see the worst of people," he reminds me. "Besides, cynical is better than sorry. You'll have tools in there, and you've already started working on the interior. I don't want anyone to break in and vandalize your stuff. I'm a little protective of my sister."

"It'll only be a few days," she insists. "Don't worry so much. You hover."

"I'll have extra patrols in the area over the next few days, just in case. And I do not hover."

"Ah, sibling rivalry," I say, blowing out a breath. "Good times."

Above us, the crane starts to move, and I can hear a saw revving up. It sounds like they're about to start taking out some of the windows.

"Looks like someone brought in pizza," Cullen says with a grin, pointing to the pizza boxes being passed around the crowd across the street. "It's not even close to lunchtime."

"I'm surprised there's no popcorn," June adds, smiling at Harvey as he jogs across the street with a box for us. "You didn't have to do this."

"Are you kidding? It gives me an excuse to come watch the show. This little church has been here for as long as any of us can remember, and most of us have family members buried out back. We *want* to watch the transformation."

"I guess I hadn't thought of that," June says, pulling a pepperoni off her slice of pizza and eating it. "I'm building a fence in the back to separate the graveyard from the house so the people who want to pay their respects can without feeling as if they're walking through private property."

"I know that we'll all appreciate that," Harvey replies as he pats June on the shoulder. "I'd better get back to the safe zone. Let me know if you need anything."

"I will. Thank again!" He hurries back across the street, and Cullen reaches for a slice of pizza.

"I eat pizza for breakfast all the time."

"Who doesn't?" I ask, biting into a piece and then turning to June. "Are you sure you want people just walking around in your backyard whenever they want?"

"No," she admits and licks her finger. "But there has to be a way that I can make it work because, like Harvey said, a lot of people are buried back there. Sure, some no longer have family living here, but some do. I don't have the time to figure out a visitation schedule or something."

"Adding the fence will help," Cullen says. "Just make

sure you keep it locked and put up some cameras for added security."

"I already plan to," June assures her brother before tilting her head and adding, "Maybe I'll get a big dog. I've been thinking about it anyway, having a big ol' dog that I can take to job sites with me. Maybe I'll rescue one."

"Not a bad idea."

The men come out of the chapel, and it looks as if the last of the windows have been taped up, which means the messy work is about to start.

"Here we go." June closes the pizza box and shoves it at Cullen. He just shrugs and moves to set the leftovers in his passenger's seat. "I'm *so* ready for this."

EVEN WITH JUNE and me jumping in to help the crew, it was well past dinnertime before the last window was out, packed, and loaded onto the truck. When we finally left the chapel, we were both filthy and sweaty, but now that I'd showered, all I wanted to do was call her and see if she wanted to grab something to eat with me.

Before I can, though, my phone pings with a text from my sister.

LUNA: *Pack a bag for the weekend and come to the inn.*

I scowl.

Me: What??

Luna: Just follow orders for once! No questions. Do it now!!!!!

"WHAT IN THE hell are you up to?" I mutter as I follow orders *for once* and pull out a duffel bag, toss in enough stuff for a couple of days, and then head toward the inn.

I didn't hate growing up out on the cliffs, but I didn't love it like Luna did. From an early age, I knew I wanted to be in town where all the action was because I didn't enjoy the feeling of isolation that came with being at the lighthouse.

Luna thrives there, though, and she's an excellent lightkeeper.

She'll be an excellent innkeeper, as well.

I park next to Tanner's vehicle, noting June's truck not far away, and then head inside.

It isn't hard to figure out where they all are since I can hear laughter coming from the kitchen, so I head toward it.

They say that you choose your family, that it's not always blood that links people together. I can say, without a shadow of a doubt, that it's true. Yes, Luna is my sister, but the others are my family because I've chosen it.

The six of us spend a lot of time together as a group, and I wouldn't have it any other way.

"You're here," Luna says when she sees me at the entrance to the kitchen.

"I was under orders," I remind her and smile when

she throws her arms around me and gives me a big hug. "Hey, Luna bug. What's up?"

"Now that you're all here, I'll tell you. I want the first people who stay here to be *you*. And Wolfe and I, of course. The six of us are the first guests of Luna's Light. Mira made us dinner, which is already waiting for us in the oven, and she'll be back in the morning to make us breakfast."

"We get to stay the night?" Sarah asks, already bouncing on her feet in excitement, her blonde hair dancing on her shoulders.

"You're staying the *weekend*," Wolfe corrects her. "Zeke will join us tomorrow night. He's busy tonight."

"This is so freaking awesome," June says with a grin as she fist-bumps Sarah. "Do we get to pick our rooms?"

"Nope!" Luna replies, shaking her head. "I kind of designed the rooms with you guys in mind, so I want everyone to stay in the room that is kind of theirs."

"Which room is ours?" Sarah wants to know, as Tanner grins at her. The man is so gone over her that they should be the center of a Hallmark movie.

"You have the Rose room." Luna claps her hands with excitement. "Apollo has the Lighthouse room."

I lift an eyebrow. "Really?"

"Of course. It's masculine and decorated in gorgeous, rich colors. It's one of my favorite rooms."

"Aren't they *all* your favorite?" Wolfe asks her.

"Hush," Luna replies, planting her hand over Wolfe's mouth, making us all laugh. "Wolfe and I are in the Huckleberry room."

"Why aren't you in the View room?" June demands with a scowl. "It's the biggest room with the best view, and you own the place."

"Because that's your room," Luna replies with a triumphant smile. "We wouldn't be standing here without *you*. That space is so beautiful and has such amazing craftsmanship in all the little details that it suits you, and you deserve it."

I glance over at June and smile because she looks utterly shocked.

"Wow," she says at last. "I've been dying to sleep in that room."

"I know." Luna pulls June into a tight hug. "And now you get to spend the whole weekend in it. I want to treat you and give you the whole inn experience. Though, it's a bit self-serving because it also gives me a bit of practice for when we open the doors to other guests."

"You can practice on us all you want," I assure her. "I'm in. I already took the weekend off work since this week was a shit show. You won't be able to pull me out of that room," June adds with a laugh. "That deep, copper soaking tub is *mine*."

"Let's take tons of pictures for social media," Sarah says. "And we can tag the inn and get people excited to stay here."

"Good call."

"But, first, we eat," Wolfe announces. "What do we have in here?"

"Chicken parm with pasta, salad, and bread," Luna replies. "Mira said she left a cheesecake in the fridge."

"I'm going to kiss Mira on the mouth when I see her," June declares as she opens a cupboard and pulls down plates. She passes one my way. "Here you go."

"Thanks." I wink and then pretend not to see Sarah's look of surprise. June typically goes out of her way to snark at me or flat-out ignore me, so something as simple as handing me a plate draws attention. I wait for her to say something, but thankfully, she just shrugs and continues to help Luna and Wolfe get out the food.

Once all our plates are filled, Tanner says, "We should sit in the dining room."

"Let's go," I reply, and we walk into the dining room and find seats.

A pass-through opens between the kitchen and dining room, and Luna grins at us from the kitchen side. "One of you guys want to come grab the salad and bread?"

"This is *so* cool," Sarah says as she takes the bread from Luna. "I love that the dining space can be separate from the kitchen, but it's easy to pass food through during service."

To my surprise, June chooses a seat next to mine, and dinner is fun as the six of us sit together at one table and enjoy the newness of the inn.

"I meant to come watch the windows being taken away, but the day got away from me," Luna says. "How long did it take?"

"All freaking day," June replies around a bite of bread. "They left just before you texted me to come over with a packed bag."

"The crew did a great job, though," I add. "I was worried one or more of the windows would break, but they knew their stuff."

"Yeah, the church hired the right crew," June agrees. "And they only needed me and Apollo to help a little bit toward the end when they were wrapping the windows for transportation."

"So, you were there all day, Apollo?" Wolfe asks, eyeing me.

I eye him back. "It was a big project, and I was curious how they'd do it."

"Yeah, well, he wasn't the only one who wanted to see it happen. There had to have been two dozen people hanging out on the sidewalk for most of the day. Even my grandma came down for a while. Someone let her sit in their camping chair, and she had the time of her life. She also invited everyone to her Halloween party, of course. Guys, it's only, like, two weeks away."

"I think this is the most I've heard June talk in one stretch," Tanner says with a grin.

"Shut it," June suggests. "The theme is *The Great Gatsby*, so be sure to get your roaring twenties outfits. Don't tell her I told you this because she'll skin me alive if she finds out, but I think Grandma is going to turn the house into a speakeasy."

"Holy shit, that's cool," Wolfe says.

"I know, but act surprised or she'll kill me." June sighs. "God, I'm full. Here, do you want this piece of bread?"

I accept the proffered bread and take a bite before realizing that everyone is watching us.

"What?"

"Why are you being so nice to him?" Sarah demands, looking at June. "Are you sick? Do I need to take your temperature?"

"What? No." June scowls over at me and then back at Sarah. "He just eats everything in sight, and I thought he'd want my bread. That's all."

"Maybe June's just in a good mood," Wolfe suggests, but I can tell by the look in his eyes that he knows exactly what's up. "It was a successful day at the chapel."

"Yeah, enjoy my good mood," June agrees. "And don't question it."

"Okay." Sarah holds up her hands. "I'm ready for cheesecake."

"Oh, good call." Luna jumps up from her seat. "I'll pass it through to you. I think it's already cut and everything."

"This is going to be the best weekend *ever*," Sarah says.

It's LATE when Wolfe and Luna start to lockup downstairs and the rest of us head to our assigned rooms. It's *very* convenient that my room just happens to be right next to June's, and I have every intention of sneaking into her room to spend time with her. I don't plan to sleep alone.

93

"Well," June says when we reach our doors. "Good night. I'll see you tomorrow."

"Good night," Sarah calls from down the hall and then giggles when Tanner tugs her into their room and closes the door.

Wolfe and Luna are still locking up downstairs.

"You know, I haven't seen the inside of that room," I say and lean on the doorjamb next to June.

"Liar," she says softly.

"I haven't seen the inside of that room with you inside it," I clarify, enjoying the way the soft light of the hallway casts little shadows on her face and shoulders. "Naked."

"Who says you get to see that *now*?"

"If you're telling me that I don't, I'll go to my own room." She bites her lip, and I reach out to tug it free with my thumb. "Just tell me no, Juniper."

"I—"

"Is everything okay down there?"

I turn and see Luna frowning down the hall at us. Wolfe's trying to pull her toward their room, but Luna won't budge.

"We're fine," I assure her. "I was just escorting Miss Snow to her quarters, being the gentleman that I am."

"Good night," June says and slips into her room, closing the door behind her.

"Have a good sleep," Luna says to me and then follows Wolfe into their room.

I stare at June's door for a minute. I could just go

inside, but she didn't exactly invite me in before Luna interrupted.

We've had a good evening—possibly the most civil evening of our lives, and I wonder if my pushing the idea would ruin it.

But, Christ, I want her.

"Don't overthink it," I mumble before turning the doorknob. When I open the door, June's standing on the other side as if she were about to come get *me*. "Hi there."

"Get in here," she hisses.

Chapter Seven

June

Apollo closes the door and then leans back against it, watching me with hungry, lust-filled eyes, and I'm suddenly anxious about what to do next. I don't necessarily feel shy, I'm just...unsure.

"Did they see you?" I ask.

"No." He doesn't move toward me, and his body is taut, his skin smooth over his defined muscles. I know from experience that his strong arms can just toss me about, move me wherever he wants me to go, and it's so damn hot. "You do realize that they'll find out sooner or later, right?"

I shrug a shoulder, unable to look away from him. Just by me willingly sitting next to him and finding subtle ways to touch him, they probably already know something is up. I tried to be inconspicuous because we're keeping things on the down-low, but none of them are blind.

"What are you thinking?" he finally asks.

"I—" I lick my lips, wishing I had some water for my dry mouth. "I don't think that I should have slept with you three months ago when you talked me into leaving that party with you."

He cocks an eyebrow. "And why is that, Juniper?"

I want to growl and swear in frustration, but I tip my chin up and reply, "Because it was supposed to get you out of my system, but it just made me want you more."

If I'm not mistaken, he almost looks relieved, and I'm not sure what to do with that.

"This is just awkward," I mumble and finally look away from him, shaking my head. "And probably a mistake."

"No." He pushes away from the door and slowly walks toward me. "Not a mistake, Juniper. I didn't work you out of *my* system either, not by a long shot. The more I had of you, the more I wanted, and it's only gotten more intense every fucking day. You're my last thought before I go to sleep, and you star in all my dreams. And if that weren't bad enough, you're the first thing I think of when I wake in the damn morning, too."

His voice has started to rise, so I reach out and press my hand to his chest. "Shh. They'll hear you."

"Do you think they aren't already wrapped up in each other? Trust me, honey, they don't give a damn about what we're doing down here."

"Ew." I wrinkle my nose. "I don't want to think about what they're doing. That's none of my business."

"Just like what we're doing isn't any of theirs." He continues, and I wish he would freaking *touch me.*

"Besides, you built this place and know the walls aren't thin."

"No." His hand covers mine, which is still planted on his chest, and he trails his warm fingertips all the way up my arm. "They're not thin, but still, we can't get too loud in here."

"You're so fucking beautiful." My heart stumbles at his whispered compliment, and I couldn't stop my feet from stepping even closer to him if I wanted to.

Which I don't.

"Apollo." He tips his forehead to mine, and all I can do is take a deep breath as he cups my face in those big hands, pushing his fingers into my hair and holding me gently.

"If this isn't what you want, just tell me to go." His voice is thick with need.

"I don't want you to go."

"Thank God."

His lips cover mine so tenderly that it catches me off guard. I've only been with him the one night, and it was a night of fast and hard sex, so I'd been expecting intensity. Urgency.

This isn't fast *or* hard.

When his fingers graze down my cheeks to my neck, and his fingertips lazily brush back and forth along my collarbone, I'm pretty sure my knees might give out.

Before that actually happens, Apollo is gently guiding me backward until my legs meet the bed.

"We're going to take our time tonight." He nibbles his way over to my ear and bites the lobe before gliding his tongue over that extra-tender skin just below it. The shiver that makes its way up my spine has my breath faltering for a just a second. "I'm going to savor every fucking inch of your incredible body. I'm going to make you sigh, and then you're going to scream."

I lick my lips, completely under his spell. "No screaming with our friends just down the hall."

"You'll want to scream, then." He smiles against my skin, and it's just as sexy as the kisses he'd just been pressing to my neck.

Unable to wait any longer to feel his skin, I tug up his shirt until he has to back away to pull it over his head and toss it to the floor.

"You know." I have to pause and swallow hard. "I've never been a woman to swoon over abs, but damn if I don't like yours."

His smile is slow and satisfied. "Is that so?" He lifts my shirt over my head and drops it onto the floor by his. "I love that you have little, tiny freckles on your chest." He reaches back and unfastens my bra, and I let it slide down my arms and fall from my body. "And I fucking *love* the way your body responds to me."

As if on cue, my nipples pucker under his gaze, making him smile once more.

In the soft light of the bedside lamp, we undress each other as if we have all the time in the world, and when we're finally naked, I scoot back onto the bed and pat the mattress beside me in invitation.

"Join me."

Before he does, his eyes go wide. "Shit. I forgot something. Hold on."

He hurries to the door, sticks his head out to see if the coast is clear, and then he's gone.

I'm left sitting here, wondering what in the actual *hell* he's doing running around the inn stark naked. So, while I wait, I climb under the covers, but only a handful of seconds pass before Apollo quietly slips back into my room.

"You went out there *naked*. What if someone was out there?"

"They weren't." He holds up a long string of foil packets and grins. "I had to grab the protection."

"Good idea."

He tosses them onto the table next to the bed and then climbs under the covers with me. His warm palm slides over my hip, up to my shoulder, and then plunges into the back of my hair.

"I seriously *do* love your hair."

"I don't." I gasp when he bites my neck again. "But I'm glad you do."

"There's nothing here that I don't like." He guides me down to rest my head on a pillow, and then he makes good on his promise to kiss every inch of me, exploring my body as if he's never seen me naked before.

When he spreads my legs and nudges his shoulders between them before covering me with his glorious mouth, I have to grip the covers and bite my lip so I don't cry out in pure ecstasy.

"Apollo." It's a whisper and a prayer as he makes me

feel things that no other man has ever made me feel. Then, just as my legs begin to shake, he pushes two fingers into me, makes that *come here* motion that he's so fucking good at, and I explode into a million tiny pieces.

Before I can fully catch my breath, he's petting and kissing me as he works his way up my torso, taking his time to worship each nipple. It's as if he doesn't want either one to be jealous of the other.

And when he makes his way back to my mouth and settles himself between my legs, he kisses me with more urgency than earlier.

"That was pleasant," I whisper as he breaks the kiss. His dark eyes warm and then fill with sheer deter-mination.

"Pleasant?"

"Mm. It was lovely."

"I see." He reaches over to the bedside table, tears off a condom, and then proceeds to protect us both. "I'm so relieved that it was *pleasant* for you when I made your legs shake so badly that you had to bury your face in a pillow so the others wouldn't hear you as you came."

"Is that what I did?"

He slides inside me so, so slowly.

"There is nothing like this," he groans, closing his eyes. "Nothing."

"Look at me." It's not a question, and when his eyes open and meet mine, I cradle his face in my hands and lift my hips, changing the angle just enough to make us both sigh in pleasure.

"I won't last," he mutters as he starts to move. "You're too sexy, too damn *good*."

"We have all night," I remind him as he picks up the pace. "Oh, Jesus, that's incredible."

"Better than pleasant?"

I can't help but laugh. "A little better, yes."

He was wrong. He lasts just fine and sends me up and over another peak before he groans and jerks, his own release taking over.

Finally, I pat him on the back. "You have to move. Can't breathe."

He rolls to the side, but he takes me with him, still holding me close.

"I want a soak in that tub. I wasn't kidding earlier."

"Do I take this to mean that you're not one for post-coital cuddling?"

I snort and pull back far enough to look into his eyes. "Does my personality give you the indication that I'm a cuddler?"

"No." He kisses the end of my nose without releasing me. "I am, though, so stay with me for just a few minutes. I'll even run the bath for you in return."

"You're bribing me for cuddles." I've never been one for sweet touches and snuggling up. I wouldn't know how to do those things. "Is that pathetic?"

"No." He kisses my forehead and tightens his arms around me. "It's normal. The cuddling part, that is."

"Look, pal, if you want a normal cuddler, you'll have to find yourself a different girl."

"I like this one." He relaxes against the pillows, just

holding me tightly against him as if he does it all the damn time.

Honestly, it's not so bad. I like listening to his heartbeat, and I kind of *love* the way his fingertips dance up and down my spine.

I've never been touched so much in my life, and it's not horrible.

"Are we done yet?"

He laughs and releases me before he rolls out, and I shift just enough so I can watch him disappear into the en suite bathroom. I hear the water in the tub turn on and smile in anticipation.

I've coveted that tub since the day it arrived for installation. It's pounded copper, and so big that I'm pretty sure the Olympic team could happily win gold in that tub.

I plan to relax in it until my bones are jelly.

So, I climb out of bed, tie my hair up so it doesn't get wet, and then pad into the bathroom in time to see Apollo light a candle. Two more, which are already lit, sit on the vanity.

"Candles?"

"And wine," he confirms. "There's a note from Luna, suggesting you take advantage of these while you soak."

"God, I love her," I declare and reach in to test the water, which is perfect. There's also a packet of lavender bath salts, and I add a handful of those to the steaming water before I climb in, rest my back against the end of it, and take a long, deep, satisfied breath. "Holy shit, I just died and went to heaven. Don't try to resuscitate me. I'm happier here."

He chuckles, and then the next thing I know, he's stepped into the tub with me and sits at the other end, pulling my feet into his lap.

"Hey, get your own tub. In fact, you have one just next door."

"It's fancy, but it doesn't have a gorgeous woman in it." I crack my eyes open to find him smiling at me. "Hi."

"Hey."

"Wine?"

He offers me the glass, and I accept it, take a sip, and then pass it back to him. He sips, too, and it seems this is the week for sharing wine with the Winchester siblings.

"Close your eyes," he urges.

"Don't have to tell me twice." I lean my head back and close my eyes while Apollo begins to rub the arch of my right foot. The perfect pressure of his thumb rubbing along the arch of my foot sends me straight into absolute and utter happiness. "You have good hands."

"They're kind of beat up. Comes with the job."

"Mine too. I have man hands with all the callouses and scars."

"You don't have man hands." His voice is soft and soothing, and his thumb never stops doing delicious things to that foot. "You have working hands, and there's nothing at all wrong with that."

I don't reply, and he doesn't seem to need one. I'm so relaxed. Every muscle has just let go, and it feels as if I'm weightless, completely stress free and happy.

I'm *happy*.

I'm not typically unhappy, but I don't know if it's ever actually occurred to me before that I'm satisfied the way it does right now.

I guess excellent sex and a killer bathtub will do that to a girl.

Apollo switches feet, and I let out a soft sigh.

"You can stop doing that in about three hundred years."

"Deal."

Cracking my eye open again, I take him in. He's much taller than me, so he's farther out of the water, and I can see that he's covered in goose bumps.

"You're cold."

"I'm fine."

"You're cold," I repeat and scoot back a bit. "Dip down farther. There's plenty of room."

He complies and then sighs. "Yeah, that's better."

"Silly man, you don't have to be cold just to make me comfortable."

"Your comfort is the only thing that matters to me."

Not sure what to say to that, I close my eyes again and enjoy the feel of his fingers rubbing their way up to my ankles.

"Have you always been so...*sweet*?" I ask, unable to stop myself. "Or is this just for tonight because of the sex thing?"

"You decided a long time ago that I was the villain in your story, and that wasn't true."

"It was kind of true." I sigh with happiness as his hands reach my calf. "I mean, you *were* mean to me."

"Once," he clarifies. "And you're so damn stubborn that you held a grudge about it for twenty years instead of just talking to me about it."

"I'm not a good talker."

"Clearly," he says. "Do you want me to call the guys I was with that day and tell them that I do, in fact, like your hair and they can go suck it?"

"Would you do that?"

He's quiet for a moment, so I open my eyes and find him grinning at me.

"If I knew who they were, then hell yes, I would do that, but I don't remember."

"Indigo Lovejoy was one," I reply immediately. "And, unlike the rest of you, he didn't laugh when you said what you said. I *like* Indigo. He's a nice guy."

"You have a good memory."

"Hell yes, I do."

"Who else was there?"

"Tanner wasn't there. I don't know where he was that day. There was a kid named Mark. Or Mike. Mick?"

"Mitch," he supplies. "I haven't thought about that guy in years. His family moved away in the tenth grade. I wouldn't know where to find him."

"You're clearly not a woman. We can find anyone on the internet in about ten minutes if we have their first name and cup of coffee. But it's fine. I'm just kidding."

"I'm not. I'll call Indigo tomorrow."

I laugh and shake my head. "No, don't make it weird."

"We're way past that, sweetheart."

My heart stumbles at the term of endearment, so I close my eyes again, keeping it to myself.

"If I fall asleep in here, don't let me drown."

"Don't worry. I've got you."

———

KNOCK, *knock, knock.*

I open a bleary eye and then sit up straight in the bed in a panic.

"Shit." I shove at Apollo, who's still asleep. "Wake up. Someone's at the door."

"I'll get it."

"Shh," I hiss. "No, you have to hide."

"Fuck that."

"*Hide*, you moron."

"Just crack the door open." He flings the covers over his head, and I blow out a breath, wrap myself in the robe the inn offers guests to use, and walk to the door. After taking a slow breath, I open the door just a crack.

"Hi."

Luna grins at me. "Hey. Good morning. Sorry if I woke you, but I wanted to bring you some coffee to get your day started. We'll be serving breakfast starting in thirty minutes, but you'll have a couple of hours to come down for that in case you want to sleep some more. I know we were all up late."

"Uh-huh." I eye the coffee.

"I'll just bring this in and set it down."

"It's okay. You can set it there, and I'll get it."

Luna narrows her eyes at me. "What's wrong?"

"Nothing, you just woke me up, and I'm out of sorts. Thanks for the coffee."

"You're welcome." She sets the tray on the floor, but before she turns to leave, she asks, "Hey, have you heard from Apollo?"

"Uh, no. Why would you think that? I just woke up."

"I knocked on his door, but he didn't answer. Maybe he went for an early morning run on the beach or something." She shrugs.

"Maybe he's just sleeping and didn't hear you knock." It seems reasonable enough to me, and thankfully, she nods.

"You're probably right. Okay, see you at breakfast. You don't want to miss it."

"Thanks."

I wait for her to disappear, and then I retrieve the tray from the hallway. Apollo is sitting up in the bed, his elbows resting on his knees, grinning at me like he's the cat who ate the canary.

Which is a really lame phrase, but that's totally what he looks like.

"Don't be so smug."

"I'm absolutely smug," he replies and takes a mug from the tray. "You didn't kick me out this time, and I got to wake up with you next to me."

"Hey, this is *my* coffee. Yours is outside of your room next door."

"Fine."

Naked as the day he was born, he gets up, checks to make sure the hallway is clear, and then leaves. A few seconds later, he walks in with another tray.

"You *have* to stop walking around this inn naked. Someone will see. What if Luna installed cameras in the hallway?"

That makes him pause. "Did she?"

"Not yet." I grin. "But she's gonna, so you might want to stop. Also, I didn't kick you out last time. I woke up, and you were gone."

"You told me to go."

"I absolutely did not."

He scowls over at me. "I distinctly remember you saying, *go.*"

"Was I asleep? Because I do talk in my sleep."

"No, you—" But he stops talking and then shakes his head. "Well, shit."

"Yeah, we have to get better at the communication thing."

He pours himself some coffee and takes a sip. "I wonder what's for breakfast. I'm starving."

"Me, too. Mira's making it, so whatever it is, I'm sure it'll be delicious. I'm hoping for cinnamon rolls and bacon. There has to be bacon, right?"

"Not so fast." He takes my mug away, and I glare at him.

"I've killed men for less than that."

"Sure you have, tough girl." He sets both mugs aside and then cradles my face in his hands. "How are you today?"

"Hungry."

"How are you after *last night*?"

"I'm great. Good. Doing well, thanks for asking. How are you?"

"Damn happy."

There's that word again. Happy.

"Yeah. Me, too."

"Good. No regrets?"

"Not yet, but if you don't give me back that mug, the regrets will set in real fast."

He laughs and slides his hand down my belly and glides his fingers to my center. "I have plans for you. Then coffee."

"I don't know if I like this bossy side of you." His fingers do something magical, and I gasp. "Okay, this isn't so bad."

"Let's see if we can do better than *lovely* this morning."

MARCH 31, 2002

DEAR DIARY,

Today was my birthday. Grandma had a big party here at our house and invited a whole bunch of people. It made me kind of uncomfortable because I didn't need a ton of people here to help me celebrate my fifteenth birthday. I just wanted Luna and Sarah. But Grandma was trying to do something fun and different, and she was so excited about it. I couldn't tell her no. It would have hurt her feelings.

On the upside, I got a bunch of presents. Things like movies and posters and gift cards. Luna's mom is going to have Sarah and me over next weekend to spend the whole weekend at the lighthouse, and that sounds like the best present of all. We love being at the lighthouse.

I can't really sleep tonight. It's warm today, so I have my window open, and I can hear the waves from the ocean. I like the way it sounds. It usually lulls me to sleep, but not tonight.

Apollo came over for the party. He didn't stay long. Now that he has his own car, he's not around much, which is way better for me.

Anyway, I'm going to go sit by the window and listen to the water.

XO,
June

Chapter Eight

Apollo

"This place is damn cool," Zeke says from beside me, and Wolf and Tanner nod their agreement. It's our last morning here, and none of us is in a hurry to leave. "I should have come the first night with you guys. The date I was on wasn't worth missing all of this. Was the food good?"

"You don't want to know," I inform him. "You'll just be sad. Why did the date suck?"

"It didn't *suck*," he replies as Tanner and Wolfe listen in. "It just wasn't anything special. Then I ran into my neighbor on my way home, and she's always a pain in my ass."

"Cherry Dubois is a nice girl," Wolfe replies, his voice mild.

"Cherry lives across from you?" Tanner asks.

"Yeah, and for someone who's barely thirty, she acts like she's eighty." He shakes his head and pitches his voice higher, mimicking his neighbor. ""Turn the music down, Zeke. I can't think when you blast that music like that. You burned your popcorn, and now the whole building smells disgusting. Didn't anyone ever teach you how to make it right?'"

I can't help but laugh into the mimosa Luna proudly handed me on my way out here.

"Yeah, you think it's funny because you don't have to deal with it."

"So, turn down the music and don't leave the popcorn in too long. It's not hard."

"It's the principle of it," Zeke insists. "I don't need anyone to mother me. Definitely not my neighbor. No matter how hot she is."

"So, you think she's *hot*." Tanner grins over at Wolfe. "Now we're getting to it."

"I'm not blind, am I?" Zeke scowls out at the ocean, as if he can just picture Cherry in his head, and she's on his last nerve. "If I didn't have a view like this one, I'd sell the condo and move. But I like my place, and I'm not going to let my jerk of a neighbor run me off."

"You spend most of your time at one of the garages with me," Wolfe reminds his business partner. "You aren't there enough to irritate her so much."

"And yet, I do." Zeke blows out a breath. "I guess it's just a gift. So, it's been nice to be here and not have to try to avoid her."

"If you feel like you have to avoid her, you either hate her or you're in denial about wanting to get into her pants."

Zeke narrows his eyes at Tanner. "I'm done talking

about her. The point is that the inn is awesome, and it's going to do great. It's as good, if not better, than most five-star resorts I've been to. My bathtub is ridiculous."

"Luna wanted really good tubs," I inform them. "She says there's nothing quite as luxurious as an awesome bath, and I think she's right. The female guests will dig it."

"So, speaking of women," Wolfe says and looks my way, "is something going on with you and June?"

All eyes are on me as I take another sip of my mimosa, trying to decide how to answer. Do I *want* to confide in my best friends?

June wants to keep things just between us for a while. I don't agree with it, but I don't want to break her confidence, so I just shake my head.

"Nope. What makes you ask that?"

"Because I'm not blind," Wolfe continues. "Something is different."

"Nope, nothing different. She's her usual sarcastic self."

That, at least, is true.

"Hey, guys." Sarah calls out as she and Luna walk out the sliding glass door, each carrying a tray. "We have some pastries for you to try that Mira wants our opinions on."

"I'm still full from breakfast," Wolfe says as he pats his flat stomach.

"I won't pass it up." Zeke takes a plate from the tray and pops what looks like a small muffin into his mouth. After he swallows, he sighs in happiness. "Luna, can I just move in here? I will happily pay rent. I'll even earn my keep. I'm handy to have around."

"Don't worry." My sister laughs. "I'll keep you guys well stocked with this stuff."

"Not me," I inform her. "I'll have to run about twenty miles to work off what I've already eaten."

"He's watching his figure," Tanner says, and I flip him off.

That only makes him laugh harder.

"Where's June?" I ask Luna.

"She's plating the lemon and peanut butter cookies to bring out."

I nod and stand.

"I'll go help her."

Ignoring Wolfe's gaze, I walk inside and close the door behind me. And there she is, at the counter, arranging little cookies on the tray.

"What do you need?" she asks me.

"Just came in to help you carry this out there."

Her eyebrows raise, and she glances over my shoulder to the others sitting just ten yards away on the patio.

"They can't see in." I wrap my arms around her waist from behind, pulling her to me. "There's too much glare on the door, so now I get a few minutes alone with you."

"They could walk in at any second."

"And, thanks to the glass door, we'll be able to see them come this way. Handy, isn't it?"

She turns in my arms, and before she can protest, I boost her up onto the countertop so she's almost even height with me.

"I don't want to sit on those delicious cookies."

"I moved them." Nibbling on her neck, I make my way down to her shoulder as I nudge her T-shirt out of my way. "You're way more delicious than those cookies."

"Right." She snort laughs. "Seriously, we shouldn't do this here."

"Says who?" I kiss my way up the other side of her neck to her ear. "Because I don't see anyone telling me not to."

"You're incorrigible." She laughs and then sighs when my mouth returns to hers. I sink into the kiss, enjoying every bit of her.

Finally, she presses her hand to my chest, giving me the clue that it's time to back off.

"We could disappear back upstairs. They wouldn't miss us."

June scrunches her nose. "I think the rooms are already being cleaned for the guests coming later."

"Damn."

Now she laughs as I step back and let her hop off the counter before she passes me the tray.

"You can carry these, and I'll grab the pitcher of mimosas for refills."

Outside, everyone is laughing, and both trays that Sarah and Luna brought out are empty.

"I guess those were good," I say as I set down my tray. "So I get first crack at these."

"You snooze, you lose," Wolfe says as I take the same seat I was in before.

June chooses a chair about six feet away from me, and

deciding that she's too far away, I reach over, grab the leg of the chair, and simply pull her closer, effectively positioning her under an umbrella.

"There, now you won't burn."

"How chivalrous of you," Sarah says with a grin. "You two have been really nice to each other while we've been here. It makes me wonder if we're in an alternate reality."

"Nah," June says, shaking her head. "We just called a truce for the weekend. I'll go back to calling him an idiot later."

"Darn," Sarah says, and she looks genuinely disappointed. "I like it when you get along."

"And I like it when he's not an idiot," June adds, which has us all laughing.

I want to pull her into my lap and kiss the hell out of her in front of everyone so that it's clear we're together. It might also show her that I want more with her than just fucking around together behind their backs.

But she hasn't given me the green light to do that yet.

"These cookies aren't the best," Luna decides, looking at a lemon cookie. "Which is shocking because Mira never misses."

"Everyone misses sooner or later," Wolfe replies and takes her cookie, bites into it, and frowns. "Yeah, this one isn't great."

"The peanut butter ones are to die for," June adds and grabs another. "Thanks for these last couple of days, Luna. It's been awesome. If your guests get even a quarter of the treatment you've given us, you'll be booked out for *months.* This will be the new it spot on the Oregon Coast."

"Let's put that out into the universe and make it true," Luna replies with a laugh. "Because that's my goal."

"There's no way this won't be a huge success," I assure her with a wink. "It's incredible."

STAYING at the inn for a couple of days made me feel like I was on vacation, and getting back to work wasn't easy.

But being on a job site with Juniper Snow makes it a little easier.

"There is *no smoking* on any job site," June says, her voice rising as she points her finger at one of her crew. He's a new kid, around twenty, who just moved into the area. I think his name is Josh.

"But, Boss," Josh says, ignoring the look on her face and the way his coworker shifts from foot to foot nervously, "we're *outside.* There are no walls in here yet, so it's not like it's going to stink up the place."

"Aside from the fact that you're *wrong,*" she replies, her voice terrifyingly calm, "just whose job site are you on? Who signs your paycheck?"

"You do," Josh replies with a scowl. "And you never let any of us forget it either. Women are such a pain to work for."

She might kill him. I cross my arms over my chest, enjoying the show.

"Is that so?" June smiles and nods as if she's giving his comment some thought. "Well, then, you no longer work for this woman. Take your shit and get off my site."

Good girl.

"What?" Josh's face turns mutinous. "Are you fucking kidding me? You can't fire me just because I said that. I can sue your fat ass for wrongful termination."

Now, *I* might kill him.

"I can fire you because you've been smoking on my sites, which is in violation of the contract you signed when I hired you. Aside from that, you're insubordinate, you're lazy as hell, and I've had more than one of the other guys tell me that they've had to fix your screwups. You've been hanging on by a thread as it is, and you know it. So, go find someone else to put up with your punk-ass shit."

"Fuck you," Josh snarls and turns to stomp away. "I don't need you. Hell, I was doing *you* a favor by staying on so long!"

"Great, no more favors for me. I'm crushed." June blows out a breath as Josh starts the growly engine of his muscle car, and then we all watch as the kid speeds away. "Well, that's one problem solved."

"Sorry, Boss," Rob Nelson, one of June's longest-standing employees says as he shakes his head. "I told that little punk that he was going to get fired if he didn't stop his crap. He didn't believe me."

"Well, now he does. Let's move on with it, okay?"

"You got it."

Rob nods, and when he walks off to get back to work,

June turns and startles, surprised to find me standing here.

"Gotta say that I never liked the kid."

"He's too arrogant for his own good."

"He's an asshole."

"That, too." She wipes her hand over her forehead and then shrugs. "Now he's gone."

"He's not your responsibility."

"Yeah, I know. What are you doing here anyway? I thought my crew was the only one on-site today."

"No, I had another job cancel, so I moved this one up." I take a step toward her, wanting to tuck the flyaway hairs behind her ear, and she holds up her hand, stopping me. "What?"

"No funny business on a job site."

"You have no idea that I was going in for some funny business."

"I see the look in your eyes. I know what that means."

"I don't have a look." I step toward her again, and she takes one back.

"Yes, you do, and you can just forget about it. I'm not kissing you here. It's unprofessional."

"You're the boss," I point out. "No one's going to care. Besides, no one can see us."

"There are eyes everywhere," she hisses, stepping out of my reach.

"Hey, Boss," Rob calls down from upstairs. "Is Apollo bothering you?"

Her lips tug into a satisfied smile. "No, he's not. Thanks, Rob."

I prop my hands on my hips.

"See? Eyes everywhere," June whispers. "So, keep your grabby hands to yourself, Winchester."

"I can't help it if you're so damn beautiful I want to touch you pretty much twenty-four seven."

She blinks rapidly, and her lips part as if she's going to say something before pressing them into a tight line. I enjoy the moment because it's not often that Juniper gets flustered.

"Stop being charming."

"Why?" God, she's adorable.

"Because I said so." Her gaze falls to my lips, and her tongue pokes out to lick her own, and I take an immense amount of satisfaction in knowing that she's as attracted to me as I am to her.

"I have to go." She turns to gather her things.

"Off to another site?"

"No, I have that meeting with Sally and Fred Newkirk about the property that asshole Eric wants to buy."

I raise an eyebrow and immediately shift my day around in my head. "I'm coming with you."

"You don't have to do that. In fact, *why* would you do that?"

"Because I don't want you to go alone."

Just when I think she'll roll her eyes at me, a soft smile touches the corner of her lips, and she shrugs.

"Okay, you can come. Do you know Sally and Fred?"

"Do I look like I just moved to town?" I think that

punk kid she just fired is the only person within twenty miles that doesn't know who they are.

June looks me up and down, taking her time with it. "Point taken."

"Let's go, then."

"I'll drive." June tosses over her shoulder as she walks to her truck and unlocks the doors. "And then you'll be my hostage."

"Hostages are held against their will," I remind her as I climb into her truck. "I'm here voluntarily."

Since Huckleberry Bay is such a small town, it doesn't take us long to drive over to the assisted living place where Fred and Sally live now, and when we walk inside, the receptionist smiles at June.

"Hey, Mavis," June says. "I have an appointment to see Fred and Sally."

"Sally called down and told me you'd be coming. You can go on up." Mavis glances my way, and her smile widens. "Hi, Apollo. I like that shirt on you."

June rolls her eyes and stomps away, but I just smile at Mavis and offer her a nod. "Thanks. Have a good day."

"Does it ever get old?" June asks once the elevator doors close.

"Does what get old?"

"You know." She waves her hand in the air as if gesturing toward Mavis. "Being ogled everywhere you go."

"I don't think that's necessarily the case."

She cuts me a side-eye look of annoyance and taps her foot.

"No," I decide after a moment. "It doesn't get old."

"You're so ridiculous," June says, and when the door opens, she hurries ahead of me. I catch up to her quickly, pull her to a stop so her back is pressed to my front, and bury my lips in her hair next to her ear.

"The only one I'm looking back at is you, Juniper. Don't forget that."

She clears her throat, takes three steps forward, and raises her hand to knock on the Newkirks' door. Only, before she makes contact, the door swings open.

"Well, June," Sally says with a happy smile. Her hair is as white as snow, and even though she's just a tiny thing, she looks healthy as can be as she opens her arms in an invitation for a hug. "Come in, dear. And you brought Apollo. What a lovely surprise."

"He asked to come along," June says as she hugs the little woman. "How are you, Sally?"

"I'm fit as a fiddle. Fred is soaking up some sunshine on the balcony. Why don't we join him?"

"Sounds good. How is he?" I ask, and some of the enthusiasm from just a moment ago falls from her face.

"He's getting by," is all she says as she leads us through the small apartment to the glass door that opens out to a little balcony. It has a great view of the mountains in one direction and of the ocean in the other. "Fred, honey, June is here, and she brought Apollo Winchester with her."

"Oh, good." Fred turns and tries to get up, but I hurry to shake his hand and keep him in his seat. Fred's health took a turn for the worse last year, and the couple made the decision to move into the assisted living facility so Sally would have help if she needed it. "It's good to see you."

"You, too," I reply. "It's a beautiful day to sit outside."

"That it is. Never get tired of the sea air." Fred gestures for us to sit, and once we do, Sally smiles at June.

"What can we do for you, dear? Is everything all right at the chapel?"

"Oh, yes. It's great, actually. When I have some more work finished, I'll have to take you over there so you can see all the progress."

"We'd like that," Fred says.

"I actually came to talk to you about another piece of property," June continues. "The lot next door to the chapel with the two abandoned buildings on it."

"Oh, we've had a few offers recently to buy that," Sally says. "In fact, one young man has been very insistent."

"I told her to just sell it," Fred adds. "We don't need it."

"Is his name Eric, by any chance?"

"Yes, that's him. He's from the city, and he's not terribly friendly, but he offered a good amount of money for the property."

"Sally," June says, leaning in, "I had a conversation with Eric recently, and he told me about his plans for that property, as well as the rest of the town."

Systematically, June tells them everything she knows about what Eric plans to do. Hearing it again makes my blood boil, and I can tell by the looks on Sally's and Fred's faces that they feel the same way.

"I *knew* something was off about that man," Sally says when June finishes. "What do you suggest, June?"

"Well, I would like to buy it from you. One reason being that I don't want Eric, or any other developer, to get their hands on it, but another is that I'd like to restore the existing buildings and rent them out."

Fred and Sally share a glance.

"I like the idea of the buildings being restored," Fred says slowly. "I was born in the house closest to the street."

"I didn't know that," I murmur, but I feel like maybe I should have, considering everyone at this table has deep roots in Huckleberry Bay.

"Of course," Fred continues, "those buildings are in rough shape. I don't know if they're salvageable."

"I would like the chance to try, and if they're not, I could rebuild them, keeping the same style as the originals. I don't want to build a huge bed-and-breakfast or hotel. I want it to look like it always has and still be functional."

"Sold," Sally says, slapping the table.

"We haven't even discussed the price," June says, letting out a surprised laugh.

"I'll sell it to you for a dollar," Fred says.

"I don't think that's allowed anymore." I shake my head, grinning. "But I know that June would pay fair market value. Hell, maybe I'll go in on it with her."

"A joint business venture," Sally says with a happy sigh. "Oh, that's romantic."

"No, it's not," June says and narrows her eyes at me, as if to say, *shut it*.

"We'll come up with a fair price," Fred says. Clearly, his mind is already made up. "If we're going to sell, I want it to be to June, and to you, Apollo, if you want in on it. I know that you'll make it special."

"Thank you," June says. "This is going to be *awesome*."

Chapter Nine

June

"This is a lot of liquor, Grandma."

I've just hauled the last of the wooden cases of alcohol into her dining room, which is where the bar will be set up for the speakeasy.

"Most of it is for decoration," she informs me, her eyes bright with excitement. "That whole wall will be shelves of liquor, and the bar will be in front of it."

"There's a window there," I remind her.

"It's getting covered up," she says, shaking her head. "This isn't your first Halloween party here, June. You know that the whole house will be transformed. I have a reputation to uphold."

"Right." I nod and smile over at her. "Did Lauren text you this morning?"

"Yes." She doesn't meet my eyes and busies herself with looking through the bottles. "She says she's coming for the party."

"I'm so excited to see her. She hasn't been home in a couple of years, and it'll be really good to spend some time with her."

"Your sister could have come home at any time," she reminds me. "She chose not to."

I know that it hurt my grandmother's feelings when Lauren decided that small-town life just wasn't for her and moved to Las Vegas after college. Grandma thought we'd all stay together, especially after the shit show with my parents, but Lauren is her own person and should do what makes her happy.

"She just wanted a different life," I say softly, but Grandma's lips tighten. "It doesn't mean that she doesn't love us or that she isn't grateful to you."

"I don't need anyone's gratitude," she insists, shaking her head. "As long as you kids turned out to be good people, that's all that matters."

"We did. Cullen's a cop, for crying out loud. I own my own company, and Lauren's one of the most sought-after architects in Vegas. I'm really proud of her."

"She's doing well," Grandma agrees. "All of you are, and I'm glad."

"But you won't admit that it'll be good to see Lauren for a few days." She just moves to the next box to inspect the bottles, and I blow out a breath. "Okay. I'll get her room ready for her."

"I'll handle that later. We have other work to do before the crew gets here later today to start the big trans-formation."

"I have to leave in a little while," I inform her and cringe inside when she turns to me with surprise on her sweet face. "Grandma, I'm still trying to get the chapel ready for me to move into before Christmas, and I have deliveries coming today that I have to sign for. Not to mention, I'm having the windows installed so Cullen doesn't yell at me again for having the plastic coverings up for too long."

"Fine." She waves me off. "I'll handle this myself. I've been doing it for years."

"What's wrong with you today?" I demand. "You're being grouchy and acting like I've done something to hurt your feelings, but I don't know what that could be because I've hardly been here lately."

"Exactly." She whirls around and pins me with the same stare that's put fear in me since I can remember. "You're never here. You've decided that new chapel project and whoever it is that you're sleeping with are more important than being here."

"I'm not—"

"Oh, don't even try to deny it. I may be headed for elderly status, but I'm not stupid. You haven't slept in that bed upstairs in I don't know how long."

It's going on a week since we all stayed at the inn for the weekend. I've been at Apollo's place every night this week because we just can't keep our hands off each other. I hadn't realized my absence bothered her, but clearly, it has.

"I miss you, too. If you'll give me ten minutes to

straighten out a couple of things," I continue, "I want to take you somewhere."

"But the crew will be here soon."

"And they've worked with you for decades, so I'm sure they already have their marching orders. A couple of hours won't hurt anything. Go get ready to leave."

Instead of arguing, she smiles and hurries down the hall to the coat closet to grab her things, and I pull out my phone and call Rob.

"Hey, Boss," he says.

"Hey, Rob, I need a favor. I can't make it to the chapel to oversee the window installation, and I was hoping you'd be able to swing over there. I might be able to make it toward the end, but I have something I need to do, and—"

"No problem," he says, cutting me off. "What time do I need to be there?"

"Around two. I can forward you the email with the work order in case you need it."

"Send it over and take care of what you need to. I've got this handled."

"You're the best, Rob. Thank you."

"No worries."

I end the call and then shoot Cullen a quick text before joining Grandma at the door.

"Where are we going?" she asks.

"Somewhere we haven't been in a long time. Too long, if you ask me. Should we take your car or my truck?"

"Your truck is so high off the ground," she says. "You can drive my car."

"Deal."

As I drive, Grandma watches the scenery go by, her hands clasped in her lap. Annabelle Snow is infamous and well-liked in Huckleberry Bay. She's quirky, with bright outfits and thick, red glasses that look so glossy against her white hair. She's outspoken and loves to gossip about anyone and everyone in town.

And she knows *everything*.

I'm proud to be her granddaughter.

"Things sure are changing," she says, still looking out the passenger window. "Just look at all the new houses popping up. I remember when all of this was countryside."

"Huckleberry Bay is becoming a tourist town, Grandma."

"I know it, and I also know that it's good for you young people who have to make a living. But I would be lying if I said that I didn't miss the days of my youth here in this little seaside village. It was a beautiful place to grow up."

"It still is. Just wait until you see Luna's inn. It's incredible."

"Thanks to you." I glace over and see her smiling at me with so much pride, she might burst with it. "You're a talented woman, June."

"Thank you." I don't know if she's ever told me that before. I know that she loves me and is proud of me, but Grandma isn't the mushy type. "I hope you're hungry."

"I worked up an appetite this morning."

"Good." I pull her car into a parking spot in front of Gordy's Diner and cut the engine. "I'm in the mood for a cheeseburger."

"Now, that sounds like a treat."

When we walk inside, I wave at Sunny, who has worked here as a waitress for more than thirty years, and then find a booth for me and Grandma. As we're taking our seats, Cullen walks through the door, and I flag him down.

"Are you telling me that I get to have lunch with two of my favorite people today?" Grandma says with an excited smile.

"That's right," Cullen replies and kisses her cheek before sliding into the booth next to her.

I sit across from them and wiggle out of my jacket as Cullen helps Grandma out of hers.

"She was being a tyrant this morning, so I sprung us both from Halloween duty and decided we needed sustenance," I inform my brother.

"The work has to get done," Grandma says defensively. "Everyone in Huckleberry Bay expects something special from my parties, and I'll be damned if we don't give it to them."

"We have a week," Cullen reminds her, but Grandma shakes her head.

"Every second of this week will be busy, but it's always worth it in the end."

"Well, Miss Annabelle," Sunny says with a smile as

she comes to a stop by our booth. "You look fantastic today."

"Oh, I've been working and didn't have a chance to freshen up." She fusses over her hair but looks pleased by the compliment. "My grandkids are treating me to lunch."

"Isn't that fun?" Sunny asks, still beaming as she turns to me. "Do you know what you're having?"

"I'll have my usual—cheeseburger with onion rings and a chocolate shake." I grin over at Grandma. "I'll work off the calories on this party."

"Make that two," Cullen says.

"Three," Grandma echoes, and Sunny laughs.

"Well, you guys are easy. Coming right up."

She hurries away, and I catch Grandma looking around the diner.

"Who are you looking for?"

"No one in particular. I just like to see who's out and about. Did you know that Indigo Lovejoy is seeing a woman he sold a house to earlier this year?"

"I hadn't heard," I reply with a laugh.

"I always hoped you'd end up with Indigo," Grandma admits, and Cullen smiles.

"Why is that?" I ask.

"Because then your name would be Juniper Lovejoy. Isn't that just lovely? And he comes from a wonderful family."

"Sounds like he's taken," I reply. Cullen chuckles, but the joke's on him. "Now, who should Cullen end up with? Indigo has two sisters, doesn't he?"

"Montana Jericho, the owner of Huckleberry Delight."

Cullen stares at Grandma and then frowns. "Why Montana?"

"Because then she'd be Montana Snow. How fitting is that?"

"I love how Grandma just pairs people up based on their names," I say to Cullen, who's shaking his head. "Maybe you should ask out Montana. She's single."

"I'm single, too, and happy that way," Cullen shoots back. "Let's not ruin this awesome lunch with talk about who we're dating, okay?"

"I'm just saying that Montana is smart as a whip, runs that ice cream shop, and she's pretty."

"She *is* pretty," I agree, loving how uncomfortable my brother is. "You'd make gorgeous babies."

"I want great-grandchildren," Grandma announces, and Cullen moves to stand.

"I'm out of here."

"Okay, okay." I reach for his arm, laughing. "We'll stop. No more talk about pretty girls and babies, I promise."

"What else should we talk about?" Grandma wants to know as Sunny returns with red baskets full of food and big chocolate shakes. "Well, this will feed me for a week."

"Don't worry, we have to-go boxes if you need one," Sunny says with a wink before hurrying off to help another customer.

"I bet you can put all of that away," I say before I take a bite of my burger. "You're a little thing, but you've always had a good appetite."

"I'm going to give it a shot," she says, rubbing her hands together. "Thanks for this, both of you. I've needed to spend time with you."

"We should make it a weekly date," I suggest. "A weekly lunch, just the three of us."

"I'm in," Cullen says, and it looks like Grandma might cry.

"I would love that." Then she takes a bite of her burger.

By the time I get to the chapel, they're putting the finishing touches on the last window, and Rob's standing out on the sidewalk, his hands on his hips, watching.

"Wow, it looks great." I offer him the cup of coffee I got for him from The Grind because I know it's his favorite.

"They were idiots," he says in that no-nonsense way he has, accepting the coffee with a nod. "Is this decaf?"

"Yes, because it's three in the afternoon, Rob."

"You're as bad as my wife."

I laugh and go to inspect the work before signing the paperwork that says the job was done to my specifications. The crew packs up to leave, so Rob and I head inside.

"Wow, it's so much brighter in here!" I turn a circle, shocked at just how much light is coming in through the windows.

"It's definitely much better this way," Rob agrees. "I see you've started to frame in some rooms. Why don't you have the crew come in and help you? We can bang this out pretty quickly if we all work together."

"I can't afford you guys." I shrug when he just stares at me. "I can't afford to pay you what I normally pay you for our regular jobs. Besides, I can get it done myself. It'll just take some extra time."

"Fuck that, June. Jesus, I've been with you since you started this company. You can ask for favors, you know."

"This is a business, Rob."

"Are you saying that we're not friends?"

The hurt in his voice brings me up short, and I shake my head. "Of course not. I definitely consider you a friend, and I trust you implicitly, but that isn't what this is about. I just don't feel like it's right to ask you to help me for free."

"You tell me when you're working on this place, and if I have the time, I'll come give you a hand. I know some of the other guys would, too. We care about you, Boss. You don't have to do this by yourself."

Damn if that doesn't make me emotional.

"Well, thanks."

"Don't start with the waterworks," he says, but he's smiling, and his voice is calm. "You plan on moving in by spring?"

"Christmas."

Rob lets out a snort of disbelief. "And you weren't going to ask for help? Are you a glutton for punishment? When did you plan to sleep?"

"I'll sleep when I'm dead." He doesn't laugh, so I shrug. "I don't know, Rob. I've been excited to build my own home, you know? I'd like to be in by Christmas so I can have my own tree decorations without having to wait a year for it."

"I can understand that. Listen, we've just wrapped up a couple of jobs, and the few things still in the works are light enough that we can wrap up by three each day. What if we ask the guys to come here until six and put in a few hours with you? Yeah, it's a favor, but if they're petty enough to ask you to pay them, then they're jerks. Besides, you'd do it for us."

I open my mouth and then close it again. I *would* do it for them, and having just those few hours of help each day would be *huge*.

"Okay, I'll ask them, but if they say no, I won't hold it against them."

"You might not, but I will." He claps me on the shoulder as Apollo walks through the door. "Something going on there?"

"Something," I confirm quietly as Apollo approaches. "What are you up to?"

"I heard your windows went in today. Thought I'd swing by and check them out. Hey, Rob."

"Apollo," Rob says with a nod. "They did a good job, once I reminded them which order June wanted them in. Then it was smooth sailing. I'm going to head home to the wife. Thought I might take her out for dinner."

"I recommend Gordy's," I say. "I took Grandma and Cullen there for lunch, and the onion rings were especially crispy today."

"That doesn't sound like a bad idea." Rob smiles before heading to the door. "See you tomorrow, Boss."

"See you. Thanks again, Rob."

"Don't mention it."

When the door is closed behind him, Apollo reaches out and takes my hand in his. He doesn't kiss me or pull me closer.

He just holds my hand.

"How was your day?" he asks.

"Completely different from what I thought it would be when I woke up this morning." I tell him about Grandma's bad mood and our lunch with Cullen. "I feel bad that she's been lonely. I should have known."

"You're not a mind reader," he reminds me. "Now that you know, you'll make sure she doesn't feel that way again."

"That's for sure."

"You don't happen to have any leftover onion rings that you brought with you, do you?"

"No." I laugh and pat him on the arm. "Sorry."

"I'll get some sooner or later." He takes a deep breath and looks around. "What else do you have on tap for today?"

"I'm going to put in some hours here. Now that the exterior is finished, I can really dig into getting these walls up and the kitchen framed in. Rob—" I shake my head and pace away from Apollo, still a bit shaken by my employee's offer. "He says he'll help for free and that the other guys will, too."

"Okay." Apollo tilts his head to the side. "Does that surprise you?"

"Well, of course, it does. I can't ask them to work here for me for nothing."

"It sounds like he's offering without your having to ask, June. They want to help."

"That's what Rob said. I just didn't expect it. I don't ask for help like that."

"Why not?"

I move to where there's still blue tape on the floor, outlining where my kitchen island will be, and I walk on it like it's a tightrope.

"Because asking for favors sets you up for disappointment. It's just easier to do things myself."

"Juniper."

I look over at him and find him frowning at me.

"It's okay to ask your friends for help, whether it's big or small."

I blow out a breath and then decide, *fuck it.* "When I was very young, my mother made it clear to me that I was on my own for a lot of things. She was messed up, Apollo. She gave us some dude's last name, but I would bet that he wasn't really our father. In fact, I'd put money on the fact that all three of us siblings have a *different* father. Not that it matters, really.

"When she finally just dropped us off at Grandma's

Kristen Proby

house and left, I was relieved but also guarded because, what if Grandma didn't want us either? Mostly, though, I was relieved because my mom was pretty damn shitty. Have you ever wondered why I don't like to cuddle? It's because no one ever cuddled with me when I was a kid. Never. Grandma would give hugs, but she wasn't a cuddler, either. So, it's just not a thing for me.

"I know that Sarah had it far worse with abusive parents, and my mom just ignored us, but it still left a mark on me. She didn't hit us or yell and scream. She just kind of forgot that we were there and needed her. So, yeah, having Grandma there to actually take care of us was awesome, but I never let myself get so used to it that I assumed we'd always have that. I love her with everything in me, and I know now that she'd do anything for us, but for a long time, I didn't trust it.

"So, yeah, I just assume that I'm on my own with most things. Luna and Sarah are my best friends, and I know I can call on them for the little things like what outfit to wear or if I want company. But for the big things? It's all me."

He shoves his hands into his pockets and rocks back on his heels, watching me.

"Say something."

"Do you know where your mom is now?"

"She died." I shrug and go back to walking my imaginary tightrope. "Grandma told us it was cancer. Whether that's true or not, I don't know, but I did some research a couple of years ago, which confirmed she had actually passed away, just not how."

"Why would Annabelle lie about how her daughter died?"

"Because she didn't want to hurt us or to avoid rumors swirling around town from getting back to us. It doesn't really matter how she died, anyway."

"I need you to know something," he says, his voice calm as can be. "I know that we agreed that what this is should stay between us for now, and I'll stick to that until you tell me otherwise, but you need to believe that it's not just you anymore, Juniper. I'm here, and I'm sticking. You actually have a whole community of people around you who care about you and would help you at the drop of a hat, no questions asked."

"I know—"

"No, obviously, you don't. Don't insult the people who love you by shutting them out when you need them the most."

"That's not what I mean to do."

"No, but that's exactly what happens. I've watched you do it for years, but back then, it was none of my business. It's my business now."

"Why, because I'm sleeping with you?"

His eyes flash, and I immediately regret that snarky outburst.

"I'm sorry, that was uncalled for, even for me. I get what you're trying to say. I do, and I appreciate it. I'm going to accept the help from Rob and the other guys, and that's a big step for me, Apollo."

"I know, and I'm proud of you for taking it." He crosses to where I'm standing and takes my hand again.

141

This time, he leans in and kisses my forehead. "I'm always here for you, June, no matter what."

We'll see.

What if I piss him off badly enough, and he simply leaves?

"Thanks." I squeeze his hand. "Thanks for the pep talk."

"Thanks for confiding in me about your mom. I didn't know that story."

"I made Sarah and Luna pinkie swear that they'd never tell anyone." I shrug. "Cullen, Lauren, and I legally changed our last names to Snow right after Mom died because we wanted Grandma's name. We'd been using it for years anyway. Grandma made sure our teachers used Snow for us in front of the other kids, and because she's Annabelle Snow, and we live in such a tiny town, they complied. But we wanted it to be legally changed, so we did."

"I'm sure that made Annabelle very happy."

"We had a little party," I say with a smile, remembering back to that day. "She got takeout from Gordy's, and she put balloons and streamers in the house. We got to stay up as late as we wanted to watch movies together. She made it a lot of fun. She makes everything fun, and I love her a lot."

"I know you do." He drags his fingers down my cheek. "You have the biggest heart, June."

I snort at that, but he doesn't laugh with me.

"I don't think anyone would describe me that way."

"I would. I see it. I see *you*."

I take a deep breath, unable to look away from his gorgeous dark eyes.

"If you break your promise and go away," I whisper, half-afraid to admit this out loud, "it will really hurt me."

He cups my face, and I hold on to his waist.

"I'm not going anywhere, baby. You can count on it."

FEBRUARY 14, 2008

DEAR DIARY,

Sarah's gone. That asshole that decided to sweep her off of her feet succeeded and talked her into moving to his place in California. They already got married. She only knew him for a month. I mean, I get that she was sad after Tanner broke up with her, but she jumped at the first opportunity that came her way. I want to run after her and talk some sense into her, but Grandma says that we should wait it out. That it won't last long, and Sarah will come back home.

I hope she's right. She's been gone for a couple of weeks now, and there's been no word from her, even though she promised to call every day. No call, no letter, nothing.

Even her brother, Scott, hasn't heard from her, and that's not like her at all. She's such a mother hen when it comes to her brother. I'm telling you something isn't right.

I feel so helpless!

XO,

June

Chapter Ten

Apollo

"Okay, that's enough of the mushy stuff." June pushes away from me and pulls the trucker cap she always wears off her head, shakes out her red curls, and then secures them once more under the hat. "I have work to do."

"I'm here to help."

She narrows her eyes at me, and I just smile at her. "Don't let that beautiful talk we just had go down the drain, Juniper."

"Fine." She blows out a breath and props her hands on her hips as she surveys the space. "What do *you* need to do in here to get ready for the electrical work?"

"Well, I'd like to get down into that basement so I can see just how easy it's going to be to run the wires under the house and if it's worth it for you to finish the space and make it livable. If it is, and that's something you want to do, my plan might change a bit."

"Okay, down we go."

"You don't have to go down with me. You can do whatever you need to do up here."

"No, I'm curious to hear what you think, so let's do it. Besides, I don't really like going down there alone, so this works."

I grin down at her and brush my fingers over her cheek. Christ, I can't stop touching her. "Are you afraid, Juniper?"

"Pssh. No. I'm not *scared* of the basement. I just don't like it."

"Right." I chuckle as she saunters past me to open the door that takes us through the existing office that she plans to convert to the mudroom, which I really think is a good idea, and to a set of steep stairs that lead down to the basement. "Is the water table high in this neighborhood? You might get flooding once in a while."

"I don't think so," she says, shaking her head as she heads down the stairs. "I didn't see any evidence of water down here before, and it doesn't smell mildewy, you know?"

She's right. It doesn't smell like there's been water down here, which is a good thing.

It's a regular, unfinished basement with a cement floor and stud-exposed walls. A bare bulb hangs in the middle of the room, and strategically placed pillars hold up the floor above.

"If you decide to use this as living space, it would need some work." Propping my hands on my hips, I glance over at June, who has wandered over to a bookcase on the far right wall. "What's wrong?"

"Why do you think, in this big empty room, there's a bookcase over here?"

"I have no idea. Maybe it was too big to move, so they left it. You could store paint cans and stuff on it."

"I think something's behind it."

I raise an eyebrow. "Are you psychic now?"

"No, smart-ass, I just think that something's behind it. I don't know why."

She tries to move it, but it won't budge, so I walk over to help. "You push that end, and I'll pull."

"Deal." With some elbow grease and a little grunting, we manage to move the case out of the way, and sure enough, there's a door. "Looks like you were right."

June doesn't look entirely happy about that, so I do the honors of opening the door, unable to see much beyond the doorway because it's pitch-black inside the space.

"There might be a light," I mutter and feel along the inside wall. "Yep, there's the switch."

The room lights up, and June and I just stand here, stunned.

"Is that a *mausoleum*?" she demands.

"Looks that way." I step inside first, completely enthralled by the plaques that mark each of the crypts. "But they're small. No way a casket would fit in there."

"I think they're cremated," June says, looking around. "This is a place to bury cremated remains. I've seen these aboveground in plenty of cemeteries. I wish there was something about this in the paperwork so I knew what in the hell is going on. Apollo, there are people buried *in my house.*"

"Well, to be fair, people were buried in churches all the time."

"Yeah, in *Europe.*"

"Obviously, it happens here, too, because here we are. Technically, they're not in your house since we're under your side yard right now. I bet that's why they never added on to the building over here."

"What am I supposed to do with these people?" Her voice is shrill with panic as she asks me a question I don't have an answer for.

"I work with electricity," I remind her. "I'm not a coroner or a city official."

"Look, I'm fine with the dead people in the backyard. I was expecting that. But this is too much. I don't like it *at all.*"

"Okay. I get that. I think you need to call the city and find out what to do. I'm sure this can be relocated to the city cemetery, but there might be a lot of red tape to make it happen."

"If they won't let that happen, I can't live here."

"June, the graves out the back door are closer. What's the difference?"

"I don't know." She throws up her hands and walks in a circle. "It's just creepier. If there are ghosts outside, they're *outside.* These people could be roaming around the whole house."

"I don't believe in that."

"You've smelled Rose at the lighthouse."

148

"Right. She's haunting the lighthouse, not where she's buried. These people have better things to do than scare the bejesus out of you in the chapel."

She narrows her eyes at me menacingly, and I want to kiss her senseless, but knowing her, she wouldn't let me do that among the dead people around us.

"Are you mocking me?"

"No, ma'am. I wouldn't dream of it, mostly because I plan on romancing you later. Let's close this back up, and you can make some calls tomorrow."

I lead her out of the mausoleum and close the door, and June lets out a sigh of relief.

"Do you want to talk about the rest of this basement?"

"I won't be using it as living space," she immediately decides. "I'll use it as storage, but I won't be hanging out down here."

"Not even after *they're* gone?"

"Not even then," she confirms. "So, you can run the wires any way you want."

"Makes my life easier." I head toward the stairs, but when she doesn't follow me, I turn back and see that she's still staring at the now-closed door, frowning. "Are you okay?"

"I don't like it," she whispers, sighs, and then follows me to the stairs. "I guess it would be worse if they were in caskets, but still."

"If you don't want to work here alone, just call me whenever you're going to be here. I'll come over and help."

"Isn't it lame that I'm now afraid to be here alone when they were down there the whole time? Nothing has changed, so it shouldn't matter."

"You're wrong." I close the door to the stairwell, and she takes another visible breath of relief. "It *has* changed because now you know it's there, but hopefully, it won't be for long."

"I hope you're right. With my luck, the city will tell me that there's so much red tape to exhume and move them that it could take years."

"I think you watch too much television." I cup her face in my hands and pull her in for a light kiss. "Breathe, babe. It's going to be okay."

"You're right. I'll ignore it for tonight. That usually works for me. I want to get a couple more walls framed in."

"Let's get started."

"Where are you taking me?"

It's been three days since we found the bodies in the basement of the chapel, and aside from seeing June on the job, I haven't had the chance to spend very much time with her.

"Well, I haven't seen much of you lately."

"I know. I'm sorry. I've had a lot to do for Grandma with the party coming up in a few days, and work's been busy. I just crash at Grandma's in the evening."

"It's not a problem." I reach over and take her hand in

mine, lifting it to my lips so I can kiss her knuckles. "I want to spend some time with you that doesn't involve work. So, I'm taking you out on a date, but I'm not telling you where we're going."

"Why didn't you say so?" she demands. "I would have dressed a hell of a lot nicer than this."

She's in blue jeans and a green sweater, and the way she has her hair loose around her shoulders makes me want to run my fingers through it. She's even wearing a bit of makeup, and that makes me smile because June usually hates makeup.

"I like you just the way you are. You look fantastic."

"I could have looked better," she says with a little pout, making me laugh. "Where are we going on this date? Just tell me."

"Up to Lincoln City to look around town, play tourist, and have dinner. We can enjoy each other without being worried about starting rumors that you'll have to deny."

"Does it really hurt your feeling so much?" she asks, turning in her seat so she's looking directly at me. "That I don't want to announce it to the world that we're together?"

"It's not the world that I'm worried about." I merge to the right lane so a little speedster can pass me. "I just don't like lying to my sister."

"You're not lying," she insists. "You're just not telling. There's a difference."

"I don't see the difference, and I'm not ashamed of you."

She's quiet for a long moment, so I glance her way and find her frowning at me.

"I'm not ashamed."

"In my experience, if you keep something a secret, it's because you're ashamed of it or embarrassed by it."

"Maybe a person just wants to keep something fun to themselves for a while so people don't ruin it for them."

"Do you think Luna and Sarah would ruin what we have? Do you think they'd tease us or mock us or make us feel bad?"

I feel her shift beside me. "No, but I don't like eating crow, that's all."

"What's that supposed to mean?"

"You know, having to admit that I was wrong and apologize. I don't like it when I'm wrong."

"And just what were you wrong about, Juniper?"

There's that silence again. When I see the scenic turnout just ahead, I pull my truck into it, throw it into park, and turn to face her.

"What were you wrong about?"

"You." It's a whisper, but it has such an impact on me that it might as well have been a scream. She bites her lip before saying, "You. Okay? Is that what you want to hear?"

"Sort of, yeah." I take off my seat belt, unbuckle hers, and pull her over onto my lap.

"This is so uncomfortable."

"It's fine." I brush her hair over her shoulder. "I think you're amazing. I always did, but I also thought you were a pain in the ass."

"So, now I'm just amazing?"

"No, you're still a pain in the ass; it's just different now."

She may narrow her eyes at me, but she can't hold back the surprised laughter that bubbles up in her throat.

"Yeah, well, you're a pain in *my* ass," she says as she tips her forehead against mine. "I guess we can tell the others sometime soon-ish. Maybe next year."

"That's only a few months away. I guess I can wait that long. Or, and hear me out here, we could tell them on Christmas. Make it extra festive."

"But Luna's having her special holiday party, and I don't want to make that about me."

"I don't think she'll mind." I kiss the tip of her nose and then her lips, and she tightens her arms around my neck, pressing closer to me. My hands slip under her sweater, up her sides, and around to her back so they can trail up and down her spine. "I fucking love your skin. It's so smooth, so warm."

"Thanks, but I'm not having sex with you on the side of the highway," she informs me, but she doesn't stop kissing me. "No way."

"I bet I could talk you into it."

"No. Someone could see. A lot of people drive this highway." She sinks in for one last, long kiss, and then she climbs her way back over to her seat and grins over at me. Her eyes are full of fun and lust, and I wish that I had her at home so I could have my way with her.

But there will be plenty of time for that later.

"Come on, let's go." She fastens her seatbelt, but when I don't start the engine, she asks, "What's wrong?"

"Nothing." I shake my head slowly. "I just can't stop looking at you. You're so damn beautiful."

Her cheeks flush, but she frowns. "I'm a sure bet, Apollo. You don't have to flatter me."

"Whoa. I'm a lot of things, Juniper, but I'm no liar. If this is going to work between us, you need to get used to my compliments, because I don't plan to stop giving them. You are the most beautiful woman I've ever laid eyes on, and that's no exaggeration just to get in your pants. Whether that happens or not, it doesn't change the truth. Now, let's get up north because we have reservations."

"We do?" She blinks at the abrupt change in conversation. "I thought this was just a casual date."

"It's both." I wink at her, start the engine, and pull back onto the highway.

―――

"I DIDN'T PACK A BAG." June is standing in the doorway of the house I rented for the night. "I didn't know this was an overnight date."

"Don't worry, okay?" I take her hand and pull her the rest of the way inside. "We're going to enjoy the view and have some fun away from home."

She doesn't protest when I lead her to the living room and she gets a look at the view through the big picture windows.

"Wow. Ocean view. It's pretty."

"I like an ocean view. Maybe it's from all those years that I lived at the lighthouse."

"Why don't you live in a place like this?" she asks, wandering around and checking out the place.

"I may love the view, but I don't want to live this close to the ocean. The weather takes a toll on the buildings and cars, so I prefer to live in town. We still have salty air, but it's not quite as bad."

"Yeah." She opens the cabinets in the kitchen. "I agree. I know that Luna and Sarah both love living right on the water, but I'm more of a land-based animal myself. Plus, I can always visit them and enjoy it."

"Exactly. Are you hungry?"

"Hell no, you just fed me an hour ago. Why?"

"Well, you're looking through that kitchen as if you're starving."

She closes the fridge and then leans against the island with a rueful smile. "I guess I have nervous energy."

"Why?"

"Because this is the first time I've spent the night away from normal life with you. It's like a mini vacation."

"We stayed at the inn last weekend."

"Yeah, but that's like a second home to me, so it doesn't count."

"Ah, I get it." I nod and slowly walk around the island and pull her against me. "Being in a strange place with me makes you nervous."

"Yes, but not in a bad way." She turns and presses her

hand to my chest, her eyes wide. "I don't mean it to sound bad."

"I get it." I take that hand from my chest and kiss her palm. "It's just nerve-racking."

"Yeah." She swallows hard. "I know that's silly."

"Not silly." I kiss the inside of her wrist, and her pupils dilate. Yeah, the sexual tension has been high since that moment in my truck on the side of the road. "I want you, Juniper."

"Thank all the gods because I've been struggling not to jump you."

I grin and push the sleeve of her sweater up so I can kiss the inside of her elbow.

"I'm going to savor you."

"No."

That has me raising an eyebrow. "Excuse me?"

"No. No savoring or lingering or going slow. I want you to fuck me, Apollo. Right here on this island, if you're so inclined."

She pulls back and strips out of her clothes, tossing them aside. Then she returns to me, pushes her fingers into the hair at the nape of my neck, and kisses me, hard.

"We always go slow," she says between kisses. "But I want it like that night after the bar. I want it a little crazy tonight."

Unable to resist her, I lift her onto the counter and grin when the cold granite against her skin makes her squeal.

Then I drop to my knees in front of her, spread her legs, and move in to devour her.

She cries out, leaning back on her elbows and scooting to the edge of the counter. When her hand fists in my hair, holding me to her, I almost smile.

She has nothing to worry about because I have no intention of moving away from this very spot.

She's already dripping wet, her clit hard and ready for the tip of my tongue to gently move back and forth over it, playing it like an instrument.

I push two fingers into her, and her hips buck up off the counter. My free hand cups her ass, holding her up as I eat and suck and pull as much from her as I possibly can.

"Apollo!" She slaps the granite beside her hip. "Holy shit, I can't. I can't. Holy shit."

"You can." I go in for more, curling my fingers inside her over and over again until she's crying out from the ecstasy of the orgasm as it moves through her.

I glance up, and her eyes are bright with pleasure as she catches her breath.

"More," I growl and cover her completely with my mouth, pulling and sucking as she shrieks in surprise and starts to shudder once more.

"I swear to god," she mutters, but the thought dissipates as she succumbs to yet another climax. "Holy fuck."

Unable to wait any longer, I pop the button on my jeans and work them down over my hips far enough to unleash myself, pause just long enough to protect her, and then plunge into her. There is no stopping to let her adjust to me before I'm pounding in and out of her at a hard, harsh pace that has us both groaning with pleasure.

"Do it," she says, sitting up and wrapping her arms around my shoulders. "Come. *Come.*"

"Jesus," I groan and can't hold myself back from doing exactly that as her silky core contracts around me, milking me dry.

When I can open my eyes again, I'm pretty sure I haven't just had a stroke, but I see June smiling with immense satisfaction.

"Yeah," she says before swallowing hard. "Like that."

"I'm afraid of going too hard and hurting you."

"I like it a little rough." She laughs and bites my lower lip before kissing me tenderly. "If I'm being honest, I like it all the ways."

"That's comforting." I kiss her nose and then slip out of her and help her to her feet before I search for the closest bathroom. Once I've cleaned myself up, I find her redressed and sitting on the couch, watching the water.

"I never know what to do with downtime," she admits as I sit next to her and pull her against me. "Especially in the past year."

"You worked your ass off this year," I agree and kiss her head, taking a breath and drawing the scent of her shampoo deep into my lungs. "Aside from building amazing things, do you have any hobbies?"

"It used to be annoying the shit out of you." She laughs and pokes me in the ribs. "Ruined that pastime."

"I'm not sorry. What else? Do you knit? Make jewelry? Do the geocache thing?"

"No, no, and no, but I did randomly find a geocache once. I guess I just work and hang out with the girls.

What about you? Do you play any instruments? Scuba dive? Have you written the next great-American novel?"

"I used to the play the guitar very badly. I had myself convinced that I would be the next Richie Sambora."

"Who's that?"

I stare down at her, floored. "You don't know who Richie Sambora is? You know, the guitarist for Bon Jovi?"

She shakes her head.

"You know who Bon Jovi is, though, right?" I ask before singing a few lines from one of his most popular songs, but she just continues to shake her head. "Who was in charge of your musical education?"

Finally, she dissolves into giggles. "I know who it is. I just wanted to get you to sing. It's probably good that the band thing never worked out."

I can't help myself. I roll on top of her and begin the tickle attack, making her shriek and laugh until she cries out, "Uncle! Uncle!"

"You're a smart-ass, Juniper."

"Oh, yeah. I totally am."

Chapter Eleven

June

"When do we have to be out of here?" I stretch lazily under the covers of this big, fluffy bed with the view of the ocean. The way the cotton sheets feel against my naked skin is bliss that could only be made better if Apollo's hands were on me.

"In a couple of hours." Apollo's stretched out beside me, also watching the ocean, his hands tucked up under his head in a lazy pose that's damn sexy. His hair looks so dark against the white sheets. His olive skin is smooth and tight over sculpted, rock-hard abs that I like to touch way more than I ever expected to. Apollo Winchester is something to look at, and I'm pretty smug about the fact that I get to be the one to lie here next to him and stare to my heart's content. He turns his gaze to me, and he smiles. "What?"

"Not only do you have the name of a Greek god, but you also have the body of one. It shouldn't be fair."

The myriad of emotions that roll over his face is fascinating. He goes from surprise to embarrassment to satisfaction, all in a split second.

"Oh, really?" He turns toward me just as my phone rings, and I slide over to answer it.

"Hello?"

"What are you doing?" Sarah asks.

"Nothing. What are *you* doing?"

"I have a question," my friend says as Apollo tugs the sheet down to expose my breasts so he can leisurely tug at a nipple.

I brush his hand away.

"What's up?"

"Have you been hanging out with Apollo? Like, apart from the group?"

"No, why?" I glance at Apollo, and from the look on his face, I can see that he can hear her.

"Because someone said they saw you together, and I said that wasn't possible, but they insisted that they knew what they saw with their own eyeballs, and I want to know if it's true."

"You know I can't stand that man," I insist and watch as Apollo rolls his eyes.

"I don't know.... I think something's up."

"I think that you're overthinking, my friend. How's Tanner?"

"You're changing the subject. Don't think for one second that I don't know what you're doing, Juniper Snow."

"You always were a smart cookie," I reply and have to

bite my lip so I don't moan when Apollo licks his way up my shoulder. "Can I go now?"

"Yeah, okay. What are you doing today?"

"Running errands and stuff for the Halloween party." I catch my breath when his hand glides down my stomach. "Sorry, Sarah, I have another call coming in. I'll call you later."

"Okay, bye."

I click off and toss the phone onto the bedside table.

"You did that on purpose."

"Duh." He nibbles his way across my chest as his hand does amazing things between my legs. "Let me show you just how much you can't stand me, Juniper."

"Holy crap, Grandma, I don't even recognize the place."

I'm standing in the middle of what's usually the living room but is now a dance floor with a small stage in the corner.

"You sound surprised every year," Grandma says with a laugh. "I would think that you'd be used to this by now."

"You outdo yourself every year." I shake my head in wonderment at the cool draperies and all the fancy décor throughout the whole downstairs of her house. This year, because the weather is supposed to cooperate, she had the back patio cleaned up so people can sit out there to talk, eat, and socialize. "You gained some square footage out back."

"If that weatherman is lying and it rains, I'll be mighty pissed off."

"He wouldn't dare lie." I turn and smile at her. "I love it. Lauren's coming in tonight."

"I'm well aware."

"Did you get her room ready?"

"I've been busy, haven't I?"

I simply stare at her in horror. "*Annabelle Snow*. I offered to do it myself days ago, and you said you'd handle it. I believed you."

"I'll do it."

I shake my head and stomp up the stairs and into the room Lauren used to sleep in that's across the hall from mine. It's being used as a catchall for things that we mean to donate or just don't have a home for yet, and it absolutely is *not* ready for my sister's arrival.

"This is a mess," I mutter, shaking my head. "What am I going to do with all this junk?"

"What are you calling *junk*?" Grandma asks as she reaches the door. "None of this is junk."

"Pretty much all of it is," I disagree as I move boxes off the bed so I can strip it. "I can't believe I didn't ask you about this days ago. If I wasn't distracted by a million other things, I would have. I wonder if Luna has any space at the inn. We could put Lauren there for the week."

"Nonsense. There's plenty of room here."

I strip the bed and toss the linens into the hallway.

"We would have if we'd taken the time to *clean* it. Never mind, I'll do it. She won't be here for a couple of hours. I can do it."

"I don't know why you're carrying on like you are," she says as she grabs a pile of clothes and stuffs them into an empty tote. "It won't take long. There's hardly anything here."

I glance at her, at the pile of *stuff*, and then back to her. "Right. Nothing at all."

With a roll of my eyes, I carry the linens to the laundry, pop the sheets into the washer first, and then hurry back to Lauren's room, where I find Grandma paging through an old photo album.

"You were the cutest baby."

"I don't have time to walk down memory lane with you, Grandma. Not today."

"Fine." She snaps it shut and sets it on a shelf. Then, to my surprise, she digs in and helps me clear the stuff off the floor. "There's space for all of this in the attic."

"Great," I mutter and set the first box in the hallway before I pull down the drop ladder that leads to the attic. "I'm going to climb up here. Can you pass me stuff so I'm not going up and down?"

"I can do that," she confirms. "Unless it's heavy."

I sigh again and close my eyes, but Grandma can't see me because I'm already upstairs.

Without giving it another thought, I call Cullen.

"Yo," he says when he answers.

"Can you come to Grandma's and help me with a few things, or are you working?"

"Just got off. I can come over there now. Everything okay?"

"Yeah, I just need your muscles."

"It's so tough on a guy, being stereotyped all the time."

"Ha ha. See you soon."

I hang up and poke my head over the hole to let her know it's okay, but she's already scowling up at me.

"What's wrong now?"

"Why did you ask Cullen to come over?"

"Because some of this stuff *is* heavy, and I'll need the extra hands. Can you pass me that one?"

When Grandma tries to lift the tote, I can see that it's too heavy, and I shake my head.

"No, don't do it. It's okay, Cullen will be here in a few minutes."

"I guess I forgot about Lauren's room," she admits after a minute of silence. "I was so caught up in trans-forming the house for the party, I just forgot."

"I should have asked about it sooner," I reply and sit in the opening, letting my feet dangle.

When something rustles behind me, I freeze.

"Grandma?"

"Yes, dear."

"Are there *mice* up here?"

"Shouldn't be." She scowls. "Might be a squirrel or two."

"Oh, shit." I scramble down the ladder and shiver at the thought of a rodent running up my back. "We need to call an exterminator."

"That is on my list, too, but—"

"But you forgot," I finish for her as the front door opens.

"I'm here," Cullen calls out.

"Upstairs in the hallway," I call back. And when my brother's foot hits the top step, I tell him, "There is something crawling up there, so I'm not going back up. Can you put all this stuff up there for us?"

"With whatever's crawling around," he says slowly.

"Yes."

"Mice will chew right through that box."

"Squirrel," Grandma oh-so-helpfully corrects.

I rub the area between my eyes with my thumbs. "We don't have a choice, Cullen. Lauren will be here in a couple of hours, and we have to get that stuff out of her room."

"Okay." He shrugs and starts up the ladder, but when he can see into the attic, he pauses. "There might be squirrels, but there are also mice—plural. There are a bunch of nests up here."

"Shit," I whisper. "Then this stuff can't go up there."

"What do we do with it?" Cullen asks as he climbs back down and pushes the ladder back up into the ceiling.

"Take it out to my truck. I'll store it at the chapel until after the Halloween party."

"Good idea," Grandma says with a wide smile, but I just roll my eyes at her. "Now, don't you sass me, Juniper Snow."

"While Cullen and I take care of this, you call an

exterminator. Right now. I'm not sleeping another night in this house while rodents are running around above me."

"Fine." She sighs as if she's simply resigned to her fate. "Being an adult is hard."

Cullen laughs, and I just stare at her. "You've been an adult for a *very* long time."

"Watch it with the *very*," she says, shaking her finger at me. "Besides, that doesn't make it any easier, you know."

While Grandma starts making calls, Cullen and I load everything into our trucks, and then he helps me make the bed and get the rest of the room cleaned up. I vacuum, and he dusts.

It goes so much faster with help.

"This is good to go," Cullen says as we take stock of our work. "I'll go with you to unload everything at the chapel."

"Thanks." I sigh as Grandma walks into the room. "What did they say?"

"They'll be here first thing in the morning. Those critters have been up there for a while, so they won't do any more damage in one night."

"Ew." I wrinkle my nose, silently deciding that I'm staying with Apollo tonight despite it being Lauren's first night home. "Cullen and I are taking the stuff to the chapel. Oh! Speaking of the chapel. Grandma, did you know that there's a mausoleum in the basement? There are cremated people down there."

She blinks and nods slowly, thinking it over. "Yes,

now that you mention it, I did know that. Sometime back in the 1920s, the church had the mausoleum added to the basement because they didn't want to take up valuable burial space in the graveyard for the cremated remains. I'm quite sure they stopped interring people down there about twenty-five or thirty years ago, though, but we have some relatives there."

"Well, I don't want them down there. I called the city, but they said they'll have to look into if they can relocate them."

"That's pretty creepy," Cullen says. "Let's go over there so I can see it."

I laugh and follow him out to the trucks. "I'll see you later, Grandma. Call me if you need anything."

"Thanks, dear. See you in a while."

She waves us off, and when we get to the chapel, Cullen and I make quick work of unloading the boxes and totes. I decide to store it all in the old office so it'll be mostly out of my way while I work.

"You've done a ton of work in here," Cullen says after we set down the last of the boxes. "It looks really great."

"Thanks. You don't really want to see the basement, do you?"

"Hell yes, I do. Why? Are you afraid to go down there?"

"I don't like it," I admit. "You go, and I'll wait."

"You're going to send me down into the basement, where people are *buried*, by myself? What kind of big sister are you, anyway?"

"Damn it, Cullen." I stomp a foot, but he doesn't back

down, so I begrudgingly open the door and start down the stairs, Cullen right behind me. "Are you armed?"

"Who am I going to shoot, June? A ghost?"

"Maybe. We don't know."

I make it to the bottom of the stairs and flip on more lights, and then I push Cullen ahead of me and hide behind him.

"The door is over there."

"I've never seen you quite this...unnerved," he decides.

"Just wait until you see it." I walk behind him and wait while he opens the door. "There's a light switch to the right."

"Got it," he says, flipping the switch and letting out a low whistle. "There are a lot of people in here."

"I know!" I hear the despair and fear in my voice. There's even some whininess in there, and I don't care.

There are dead people in my fucking house.

"Yeah, it has to be haunted, don't you think? With all these people?"

"You're not helping." I punch him in the arm, and he smiles over at me.

"I could arrest you for assaulting an officer."

"Go ahead. It will get me out of here."

He laughs again, and then backs out of the room, taking pity on me. "Let's go upstairs, scaredy cat."

"Thank God."

Once back upstairs, I close the door and then flip the lock just to make myself feel better.

"You really are unnerved."

169

"Wouldn't *you* be?" I ask.

"Not really. I'll bet the city can help you," he replies before ruffling my hair. "It'll be okay. In the meantime, you could have someone come in and sage the place. Just in case."

"Don't think I won't. Come on, let's go back to Grandma's and wait for Lauren. She should be here soon."

"Shouldn't we get some food? Maybe we should pick up some pizza."

"Good idea. Lighthouse Pizza is her fave, but no anchovies. I don't know how you can eat that crap."

"They're good for you," he insists, making me laugh as I lock the door of the chapel behind us. "I'll pick it up on my way over since you got lunch the other day."

"Hey, thanks." I wave at him and then grab my phone, deciding that, since I have a little time with Cullen picking up the pizza, I'm going call Apollo and see if he wants me to swing by and say hello.

"Hi, beautiful."

I smile as butterflies start to dance in my belly. "Hey. Where are you?"

"I'm actually home right now. Where are you?"

"Stay exactly where you are." I start the truck and put it in gear, heading toward his place, which is just a few blocks away. "I'm coming over."

"You won't hear me complain. See you soon."

He hangs up, and seconds later, I park on the street in front of his small house. Apollo's standing in the open doorway, shoulder leaning on the doorjamb, and his arms are crossed over his chest, and I start to salivate.

He's delicious.

"I'm a mess, but I wanted to come see you for a minute," I announce as I push him inside, shut the door, and jump into his arms. My legs wrap around him, locking at the ankles, and I kiss the hell out of him.

He braces my back against the wall, moans, and returns as good as he gets, not missing a beat.

I freaking love that about him.

"You don't look like a mess," he informs me, his lips pressed to my neck. "You look damn delectable to me."

"I *am* dirty." I sigh when he bites the tender skin over my collarbone. "I've been cleaning at Grandma's, and it was dusty and dirty. I have to get back over there. Lauren's on her way down from Portland."

"I thought she lived in Vegas." His mouth finds mine again before I can answer him, and I groan in anticipation, gripping on to his hair. I freaking *love* the way his hair feels in my fingers.

"She does. She flew into Portland and is driving here from the airport."

I'm grinding down on him, wanting nothing more than to feel him inside me right now.

"Apollo," I murmur when his lips travel to my ear.

"Yeah."

"I need a quickie."

He chuckles as he sets me on my feet. "That so?"

"Yeah. I have to get back to Grandma's, but first, I want you." I easily slip out of my jeans, and as soon as I

Kristen Proby

have them off, he has me pinned against the wall again and is sliding into me, fucking me hard and fast, watching me with those hot, dark eyes.

"Is this what you need, Juniper?"

"Yes. Hell yes."

I tighten around him as the orgasm builds low in my belly.

"Shit, yes, this is what I want. Jesus, it's just so *good*."

He groans, buries his face in my hair, and pounds into me even harder than before. Then I'm falling into the sharp pleasure burning through me, and he's pushing so deep as he chases his own release that I know I'll feel him later.

I give myself a moment to bask in the feeling and enjoy the way he can't seem to catch his own breath before I slide my legs back to the floor and press a kiss to his lips.

"Okay. I have to go."

"Damn, June."

I laugh as he follows my lips for more. "For real, though. I'm sorry, I really do have to go."

"Come back later." He kisses me softly. "For the encore."

"Hell yes, I am. My grandma has mice in her attic. I'm not staying there. The others can fend for themselves."

"That's so...*heroic* of you."

I laugh and pull my jeans back on, but then pause when I see that all the color has left Apollo's face.

"What? Are you afraid of mice, too?"

"Fuck me sideways, June. I didn't use a condom. I didn't—oh, shit."

"Hey. It's okay. I've been on the pill since high school. We're okay."

"Really?"

He wipes his hand over his mouth, clearly upset by the thought of getting me pregnant.

I can't blame him. That wouldn't be ideal.

"I promise, I'm on the pill. It's *one time*. And it's my fault because I totally jumped you and scrambled your brains."

He doesn't smile back as he lowers his forehead to mine and cups my face.

"I would *never* risk you." His voice is rough with emotion. "No matter how badly I want to be inside you, I would *never* put you at risk."

"We're safe from pregnancy," I assure him, unsettled by just how knocked off his axis he is. "Until this second, we've been doubled up on the protection. We're fine."

"Okay." He kisses my forehead and then my lips. "If you're sure."

"I'm completely sure. I never forget my pill. Besides, now I get to walk around for the rest of the day and feel you there. It's kind of *naughty*."

He nods, relief written all over his gorgeous face, and then he grins. "That's hot as hell, actually."

"Should I be offended that you're so relieved that pregnancy is off the table?"

"No, you shouldn't be." He kisses me once more. "It's not you at all. I don't want an accidental pregnancy. If—

or when—that time comes, it'll be a decision we make together. That's all."

"Okay. Now that I'm completely uncomfortable, I think I'll go see my sister."

He kisses my hand, and there go those butterflies again.

"Have fun," he says. "And come over any time. I'll be here."

"Thanks. And just so you know, I'd come over even if there *weren't* mice in my grandmother's attic."

"Good to hear." He laughs and walks me out the front door. "Drive safe."

I wave and get into my truck, but for the first time since I started seeing Apollo, I regret our agreement not to tell anyone about us because I'd very much like to tell Lauren all about how amazing he is.

"I MISSED THIS," Lauren says, lifting a slice of pepperoni to her lips, just as I walk into the kitchen. "Hey!"

"What happened to you?" Cullen asks with a frown.

"I, uh, had to run an errand." I hurry over to Lauren and wrap her in a tight hug. "Hey, baby sister."

"You look *amazing*," she says as she grips my shoulders and pulls back to look at me. "You're glowing, and you just look so *happy*."

"Thanks."

"Glowing?" Grandma narrows her eyes, watching me

closely. "Yes, that's right. She's been sleeping with someone."

"*Grandma.*"

"Who?" Cullen wants to know.

"Spill it," Lauren agrees.

"No one," I reply, shaking my head and going for the pizza. "Grandma's imagining things again."

"I don't imagine anything," she mutters, shaking her head. "But, that's fine, keep your secret. Lauren was just telling us about her latest project in Vegas."

"What are you working on?" I ask before taking a big bite of pizza.

"A resort," Lauren says. "A *big* resort with an unlimited budget. It's going to be amazing, and when it's done, I want all of you to come see it."

"When will it be completed?" Cullen asks.

"Not for a couple of years, so you have plenty of time to schedule in a trip."

"I wouldn't miss it." I nod at her, but Grandma just makes a harrumphing noise and walks out of the room.

"Don't pay any attention to her," Cullen says. "She's grumpy."

"She misses you," I add. "She won't admit it, but she wants to see you more often."

"I FaceTime her every single week. What more does she want?"

"In an ideal world, she wants you to move home." I take another bite. "She wants you here in Huckleberry Bay."

"Yeah, well, that's not going to happen. I *like* living in

the city, but I'll do my best to come out here more often. At least twice a year."

"You're living an awesome life," Cullen reminds her. "Don't feel guilty about that. Grandma just misses you and doesn't understand."

"Still, I'll come home more often. Now, can we talk about how amazing this place looks?"

"Right? We still have a couple of days to go, too." I reach for another slice. "It's the biggest party of the year, and Grandma likes to knock everyone's socks off."

"Well, this year will be no exception," Lauren says with a nod. "I'm so glad I bought a cool costume for it."

"I'm glad you did, too," Cullen says with a laugh. "We're expected to play the part. If we didn't, we might get kicked out of the family."

"Not kicked out," I reply, thinking it over. "Maybe just suspended until next year."

"I still don't want to risk it."

DEAR DIARY,

Grandma's Halloween parties always kick ass, but this one was CRAZY PANTS. I swear, the whole town comes every single year, and I don't know how they all manage to fit inside of her house, but they do. This year's theme was African safari. I was a lioness, and believe me when I tell you, I was hot. Luna was a cheetah. Because we were both over twenty-one this year, we got to drink without hiding it from Grandma, and let me just say, we had FUN.

And now I have to crash. Still have work tomorrow. Isn't that lame? Oh, well.

XO,

June

Chapter Twelve

Apollo

After a few days of only seeing June late at night, when she drives over to my place, crashes, and then leaves before the sun is up, I'm ready to see her at tonight's Halloween party.

Sure, I won't be able to touch her as freely as I'd like to because no one knows that we're together yet, but at least I'll be near her, hear her laugh, and be able to enjoy her.

She didn't want me to see what her outfit looks like for tonight, so she went to Annabelle's house early in the afternoon to get ready, and I'm headed over to Luna's to finish getting ready myself and ride over with my sister and Wolfe.

All the lights in the inn are on as I bypass it and park in front of the house that's attached to the lighthouse, where Luna and Wolfe live. I knock twice and then let myself in.

"Where are you guys?"

"I'm in the kitchen," Wolfe calls out, so I head that way. He's in his suit and hat, and he's wearing those cool black shoes that have a white thing that hangs over them. I don't know what it's called.

"You look dapper," I say as he turns and takes in my own costume.

"Same goes." He grins when he spots my baker-boy cap. "I like your hat."

"I've never had a reason to wear pinstripes." I glance down at my brown suit. "But I kind of like it."

"I'm ready."

A breathless Luna marches into the kitchen, stops short, and smiles at both of us.

"You two are *handsome*."

"That dress is amazing." It's royal blue with silver sequins and silver fringe that sparkles when she walks. Her hair has little waves in it, and she's wearing a headband with a blue feather that matches her dress.

"It's heavy," she says with a laugh. "And I hate bright red lipstick, but it was all the rage a hundred years ago. Are we ready?"

"As we'll ever be," Wolfe says. "Zeke's meeting us there."

"Awesome, let's go."

We ride together so we take up less parking space, and when we walk up to the front of the house, Wolfe whistles long and low.

"I didn't think they could outdo last year's Disney theme," Luna says. "But I was wrong."

The front of the house looks like an old-fashioned

storefront. The windows advertise women's dresses for less than two dollars and men's shoes for three dollars in bold, vintage writing.

When we get to the front door, a little cutout slides open, and we can only see a set of eyes.

"What do you want?"

"Password," Luna whispers to me.

"Just looking for some candy canes," I say, and then the cutout slides shut, the door opens, and we're gestured inside. A heavy, black curtain hangs across the entrance, but when it's pulled back, it unveils one hell of a party being had.

"It's totally a speakeasy," Luna says with laughter. "We even had to use the password."

Annabelle's Victorian-style home is sprawling, and she doesn't waste even an inch of space. The bar is busy, the dance floor hopping, and people are laughing and talking in groups throughout the first floor of the house.

"You're here!" Sarah and Tanner join us, both of them dressed similarly to the rest of us, just in different colors. "This is *so* fun. They even made us use the password. I didn't think it was a real thing."

"Annabelle doesn't play around, even when she's playing around," Tanner reminds her. "Let's hope the cops don't crash the party and take us all to jail."

"Speaking of the cops, check out Cullen." I point to where June's brother is standing across the room, dressed head-to-toe in a vintage police uniform. He even has the domed helmet-looking hat and a huge handlebar mustache that looks damn uncomfortable.

"There's June!" Luna jumps up and down and rushes through the crowd to hug June before dragging her back toward us, and all I can do is stand here and stare like an idiot.

She's wearing a green flapper dress with silver fringe that hugs every amazing curve of her body. Silky green gloves cover her arms up over her elbows, and she's holding a long, black cigarette stick, complete with the cigarette. Her red hair is tucked up in a little bob, and she's wearing dark eyeliner and bright red lipstick.

Jesus, she's gorgeous.

"Wow," Sarah says, grabbing June's hand and making her spin. "That outfit is out of this world."

"Grandma expects us to go a little over the top," June says with a shrug. "Did you see Cullen's uniform?"

"It's awesome," Luna says with a nod. "How did she get an entire speakeasy in here?"

"She has her ways," is all June says. When she glances toward me, her green eyes turn hungry as they quickly skim over my body, but then she glances away again. "I'm not allowed to divulge any of those *ways* to you, either. Sorry."

"I like your dress." It's a simple statement, and I want to say much more, but there are too many people around.

"Thanks. Your suit doesn't suck at all. I'm shocked."

There she is, being sassy, and it makes me laugh.

"You guys weren't kidding." Zeke joins us, holding a glass of whiskey. "This party *is* insane. I've never seen anything like it."

"That's right, this is your first one," I say to Zeke, who

looks like he's just walked into the Met Gala. "It's a shock to the system, isn't it?"

"You have no idea." He glances to his left and then sighs. "Shit. She's here."

"Who?" Luna looks around, frowning. "Who's here?"

"Let me guess," Wolfe says with a smile. "Cherry Dubois."

Zeke blows out a breath, and Luna frowns at him. "What's wrong with Cherry? I've known her all my life. She's super nice."

"She's been faking it," Zeke says. "I can assure you she's not *nice*."

I laugh because, as he's been talking, Cherry has been making her way over to us and has come to a stop next to Zeke. "Well, look what the cat dragged in," she says, looking him up and down. "They let you in here?"

"I had the password," Zeke says through clenched teeth.

"You should enjoy yourself," Cherry continues. "The music is loud enough to make us all go deaf and there's plenty of liquor."

"Wow, she's meaner to him than I am to you," June mumbles as she steps closer to me. Everyone is too enthralled by Cherry and Zeke flinging insults back and forth to each other to notice her shift. "It's kind of fascinating."

"You're fucking gorgeous," I whisper so low that only she can hear. "How am I supposed to keep my hands to myself all evening with you looking like that?"

"Let's go dance," she suggests. "Then you don't have to."

Without waiting for her to change her mind, I take her hand and lead her out to the dance floor. Thank the gods that the band starts a slow song, and I pull her into my arms and breathe her in.

"Are you sure you want to do this?" It's a low whisper in her ear. "People will get the impression that you like me."

"It's just a dance." She takes a long, deep breath and lets it out slowly as we sway from side to side. "If people talk about a dance, they have too much time on their hands."

"We live in a small town. A dance is a big deal, but I'll shut up now so I don't talk you out of it."

We move across the floor, ignoring everyone and everything around us, and when the song comes to an end, I dip her back and watch as she laughs.

"Don't drop me," she says as I pull her back to her feet.

"I'd never let you fall."

I want to kiss the top of her head, but I hold myself back, already nervous about what everyone is going to say about us dancing. Only, when we get back to the group, it's as if they didn't realize we left.

"She's a pain in the ass," Zeke insists, still obviously talking about Cherry.

"You know, they say that if you have to insist so hard that you don't like someone, it's usually because you're talking yourself out of liking them," Luna says. "Which tells me that, although Cherry may get on your nerves from time to time, you like her."

"I'm going to get another drink," Zeke mutters and stomps away.

"Ten bucks says they're sleeping together before the end of the year," Tanner says.

"I'm not taking that bet," I reply, shaking my head. "Because I'd lose. They'll definitely be sleeping together soon. Maybe tonight."

"I don't think so," Sarah says. "She *really* doesn't like him. Trust me when I say that, if a woman has decided she doesn't like a guy, there's no way in hell she'll get naked with him."

The humor in June's eyes matches mine, but we both manage to keep from laughing.

"Damn it."

Walking into the first job site Monday morning, I'm met with the view of June's fine ass, encased in classic coveralls, as she bends over a saw.

"What seems to be the problem?"

"Shit!" She jerks up, clutching at her chest, and glares at me. "Why do you always do that to me?"

"Maybe because you're always bent over something. What's wrong with the saw?"

"Wires were stripped on it," she mutters, glaring down at the saw. "They didn't look like that on Friday."

The hair on the back of my neck stands up. "So, who was in here over the weekend and ruined your tool?"

June blows out a breath and rubs her eyes with the heels of her hands. "Probably the kid I fired last week. He should have just stolen it. Then, at least, it wouldn't have gone to waste."

"Do you have proof?"

"No." She drops her hands and props them on her hips. "Nothing else is messed with, just this. Which is weird, right? Wouldn't you think that, if someone went through the trouble of coming here to destroy stuff, they'd ruin everything? Don't get me wrong, I'm glad they didn't, but this is petty. You're an electrician. Come look at this and tell me if you can fix it."

I move past her and look over the damage. "If this were a newer model, I could probably rewire the whole saw in about an hour, but this one is older, so I'm not sure. You might be better off replacing it."

"I was going to wait until after the first of the year to do that so I could put it on next year's taxes."

I grin. "I kind of love that you think of things like that."

"Yeah, well, I guess it'll be going on this year's return. What are you up to?"

"Working and flirting with you. Two of my favorite things."

"No." She holds up her hand and presses it to my chest. "No flirting on the job. How many times do I have to remind you? It's unprofessional."

"You're the one touching me." I take her hand and kiss her palm. "Besides, I hardly saw you all weekend."

"I had to help clean up from the party, and I wanted to spend some time with Lauren before she went back to Vegas this morning. Since the exterminator came and took care of the mice and a family of squirrels in the attic, I don't mind sleeping there when I have to." She licks her lips as she shuffles her feet. "But, I can admit, I'd rather sleep at your place."

"Then I hope you'll be back tonight."

"Yeah." She nods and looks around to make sure no one's watching us. "I will. It's been a crazy morning, and I'm a little hangry, so I'd better go find something for lunch."

"Why don't you let me buy you lunch. How does the diner sound?"

"I'd give my right kidney for a cheeseburger," she says. "But it's not a date."

"Call it whatever you want, and I'll call it a date if I want to." I laugh when she scowls at me. "Come on, grumpy girl, let's feed you before you commit murder."

Fifteen minutes later, Sunny takes our order, and I sit back in the booth, watching Juniper as she looks around the diner as if she's searching for someone.

"What's wrong? Don't want to be seen with me?"

This has her looking a bit guilty as her attention comes back to me. "I'm sorry. It's so stupid. I never should have told you that we can't tell people we're together. It feels like I'm in too deep to change the rules and let the whole town see us be all mushy and kissy face. The last thing I want is for Luna and Sarah to find out from someone other than me because it'll hurt their feelings."

"Luna might kill us." Not really, but the way Juniper's eyes widen in fear is adorable. "Her brother and her best friend have been doing the horizontal mambo for weeks and haven't bothered to tell her. In fact, they've been lying and vehemently denying it the whole time. Yeah, she'll be a little pissed."

"I'm dumb." She buries her face in her hands. "I'm *really* dumb."

"Nah. You just didn't plan on catching feelings for me on top of enjoying the sex."

Her head snaps up. "I am *not* catching feelings."

"It's okay. You can admit it."

"No way. It's not happening."

I move to hold her hand, and she pulls it back out of my reach, making me raise an eyebrow.

"Good sex doesn't equate to feelings of any kind."

"No, it doesn't, but looking at me the way you do does. Wanting to spend time together does. Needing to be close to you, to hear your voice and tell you about my day *does*, Juniper. The sex is just a very fun perk."

She lets out an annoyed huff. "Well, shit. When did that happen?"

"It's been happening; you're just too stubborn to admit it."

"You." Our heads swivel as that asshole Eric storms across the diner toward us, his eyes shooting daggers in June's direction. "What did you do?"

"About what?" June's voice doesn't waver, and her

face looks bored as she looks up at the man. "And hello. It's not nice to see you. I thought you went back to New York where you belong."

"You're buying the property I wanted."

"That's a personal matter and none of your business."

"*Bullshit!*" He bangs his fist on the table, and I lean toward him.

"Watch yourself."

"You snatched that property out from under me, and I want you to sell it to *me* for what you paid for it."

"Not in this, or any other, lifetime." June shakes her head, never once dropping her indifferently deadpan look. "Who do you think you are, anyway? No one here gives a flying fuck about your money or where you come from."

"Do you think I can't make you sell?" His voice is only rising, and the other people in the diner are openly gawking now. "I'll make your life a living hell until you give me what I want."

"You can try," June says, smiling sweetly. "But, in case you're slow on the uptake, which I suspect you are, I'll remind you that I don't have to do *anything*. So, go away."

"I'll fucking ruin you, you little cunt."

My sudden appearance in front of him has him stepping back, which shows he isn't a *complete* idiot. I'm three inches taller and outweigh the little prick by fifty pounds.

"Enough," I say. "You won't speak to her like that.

Your business plan is done. Pack up your shit and get the hell out of here."

"Or what?"

"Or you and I can take it outside and I'll show you exactly *or what*. Do you think you don't have a dozen cell phones recording you right now? I'm pretty sure that your threats have warranted a call to the cops, and June's brother *is* the cops. And in case you missed it, no one's going to sell to you, not now that the whole town knows what you planned to do here. You've been blacklisted in Huckleberry Bay, man. Go find another town to terrorize. It won't work here."

He wants to punch me. I can see it in his eyes as they burn with fury, and I wish he'd try it, because I'd have him knocked out and on the floor in a fucking heartbeat.

Instead, he marches away and out the door.

"Before you say anything"—I sit back down and hold my hands up—"I *know* that you had that handled. You're a badass, and you don't need me sticking my nose in, but if you think I'll sit here while *anyone* speaks to you that way, you don't know me very well."

She starts to speak, but then clears her throat. "Okay. Well, I guess that confrontation was going to happen sooner or later. Do you think he'll leave town?"

"He'd be stupid to stay after threatening you like at. If anyone had still been willing to sell to him, which no one was, they won't be once they find out about what he just said."

"Good. He's a jerk, and we don't want him here."

"Agreed."

"Your lunch is on the house, honey," Sunny says as she sets our baskets in front of us. "If someone has to deal with the likes of *that*, they should get a free meal. Enjoy."

"Thanks! Free cheeseburgers taste even better," June says with a grin, and Sunny heads to her next table as June's eyes find mine. "And thank you, too. That was kind of hot, actually. You didn't even have to touch him, and he was scared of you."

"He was pissed off more than anything."

"No, I think if you'd raised your fist, he would have pissed himself. Does it make me a bad person that I kind of wish that had happened?"

"Maybe a little vindictive, but not bad."

Chapter Thirteen

June

"Show us what you're painting now," I suggest to Sarah. She invited Luna and me over to have appetizers for dinner and some drinks, and I admit, I needed some girl time. "You know how much I love your art."

"Oh, I have some really fun projects in the works," Sarah replies, her eyes lighting up with excitement. "Come on out to the studio, and I'll show you."

She grabs a bottle of wine and three glasses, but I hold up my hand.

"You know, my stomach hasn't been great the past few days, so I think I'll just drink water tonight."

"Oh no, did you eat something off?" Luna asks as Sarah returns one wine glass to the cabinet and pulls a bottle of water out of the fridge.

"It's either that or stress. I've been working my ass off on the chapel over the past few weeks, but Thanksgiving is this week, and I'm not even close to being done."

I follow them out of Sarah's back door, across the patio, and over to the guesthouse where Sarah has her art studio set up.

Earlier this year, she had been living in the space, having rented it from Tanner, but when she moved into the main house, Tanner set her up out here with a really kick-ass studio.

It makes sense because Tanner owns an art gallery, and he understands how important it is to Sarah to have her own space to create.

"It's so cool in here." They removed all the furniture out of the living room, there's an easel set up in one corner, and there are canvases leaning against the walls all around the room. Some are empty, waiting for Sarah to work her magic on them, and others are covered in gorgeous colors.

"It helps to have a working kitchen and bathroom out here. Tanner even insisted that I keep the bed in the bedroom in case I wanted to take a nap. You guys, I never could have even dreamed that I'd end up with a place like this."

"It's pretty damn sweet," Luna agrees with a nod as she takes in the different pieces. "I love this one."

She's standing in front of the canvas on the easel. It's a seascape with moody clouds and choppy waves, and there's a whale's tail coming up out of the water. The sand is sprinkled with crystals and starfish, and it looks as if you could walk right into it.

"Thanks," Sarah replies as she pours wine for herself and Luna. "It's not quite done yet, but it's getting there."

"I swear that I'm not crashing your party," Tanner says as he opens the back door by the kitchen and comes in carrying a tray of food and leading Sarah's one-eyed rescue cat, Petunia, on a leash. The cat happily runs into the studio and winds her way through Luna's legs. "I'm just bringing out the food so it doesn't go cold."

"Thanks, babe," Sarah says, smiling as she loops her arms around his neck and gives him a big kiss.

"Ew." I wrinkle my nose. "Save that shit for after we've left. Remember when I told you that I've had an upset stomach? This isn't helping."

With a laugh, Tanner gives her one last kiss and then walks out the door, leaving us alone with excellent food and a very happy cat.

"June, we cut you off earlier," Sarah says as she pulls some paper plates out of a cupboard and gestures for us to help ourselves to the food. "You don't think your chapel will be done by Christmas?"

"I don't see how." I shake my head and stare at the spread of comfort food. There's hot artichoke and spinach dip, bruschetta, cheeses, meats, and all kinds of olives and breads. It's an awesome-looking little buffet of goodness, so I mentally cross my fingers that my stomach won't revolt and fill my plate. "It's been three weeks since Grandma's party, and I've been busier than I thought I would be at this time of year with actual work. I haven't been able to spend as much time on my place as I'd like."

We settle on stools around the little island in the kitchen to eat.

"What do you have left?" Luna asks as she scoops some dip with a chip.

"A lot." I shake my head and sigh in happiness when the bruschetta tastes like heaven and doesn't make my stomach roll. "The walls are all done, complete with drywall and texture, but I still need to paint. The kitchen has cabinets, but they also need to be painted, and there are no countertops yet. The trim needs to be done. I need light fixtures. And don't even get me started on the bathroom and mudroom."

"What's happening with the bodies in the basement?" Sarah asks. I showed them the little mausoleum in the basement the week after the party, and it freaked them out as much as it did me.

"The city thinks that we should be able to move them —respectfully, of course—to the mausoleum for cremated remains at the city cemetery. I only have to get final approval from someone higher up. As long as no one has been interred in the last twenty-five years, it's considered abandoned."

"Oh, my god, will they have to bring them up through your house?" Luna asks, looking horrified by the thought. "Because, holy shit, I wouldn't want that."

"They'll bring them up and out the back door so they won't have to come through the whole house."

"Good." Luna sighs in relief.

"Once that's done, I'll seal off that door downstairs so I can forget that it ever existed. Cullen thinks I should use it for storage."

"No fucking way," Sarah insists, shaking her head. "No. Absolutely not."

"Agreed." I reach for more bruschetta, happy that it's sitting well on my stomach. "I'm just glad that it's not going to be a huge hassle to have them moved. But, you guys, I need to talk to you about one of the graves down there."

This has both of them leaning toward me.

"Go on," Sarah says before stuffing some olives into her mouth.

"I found Daniel Snow down there. Rose's true love that she talks about in her diaries."

"You're kidding," Luna says, sitting back in shock. "He's down there?"

"Yes. Grandma asked me to go down and see if her best friend from high school was interred down there, and it's a true testament to how much I love that woman that I agreed to do it. I found Daniel while I was looking for her and had a thought. Luna, do you remember the night that you and I were talking, and you wondered if Rose sticks around the lighthouse because she has unfinished business?"

"Yes. She seems so sad to me sometimes."

"What if she's looking for him?" Sarah interrupts, bouncing in her seat. "Oh, my gosh, this is romantic as hell. What if she's looking for him, and we know where he is, so we move him out there so they can spend eternity together!"

"That's exactly what I was thinking."

Sarah and I stare at a stunned Luna, waiting for her reaction.

"Obviously this needs to happen," Luna says at last. "Do we need to get permission for this? Because I'm absolutely fine with giving my permission for him to be buried with Rose in the family graveyard on my property."

"Well, I'm a direct descendant of Daniel, and I give permission for him to be moved." I clap my hands in anticipation. "We probably still have to file something with the city so they have a record of where he's moved to. He's been dead for roughly a century, so I don't think anyone is going to cause any problems, though. He's going to be moved anyway."

"We can move him *this week?*" Luna asks.

"Why not? He's on my property, and he's going to your property. I don't see the problem here. But I'll make sure we file all of the proper paperwork. I don't want to be a grave robber or anything."

"This is awesome," Sarah says and pours herself some more wine. "I never thought I'd ever be involved in exhuming a body, and maybe I watch way too much true crime, but it's kind of fun."

"I'm excited for Rose and Daniel to be together again. She loved him so much." Luna grins. "Something tells me this is exactly what she needs."

"Then we'll do it."

"You're doing *what*?" Apollo props his hands on his hips and stares at me as if I just told him I'm moving to Antarctica.

"We're moving Daniel Snow to the lighthouse cemetery today." I grab a jacket from Apollo's closet. Over the past month, several pieces of my clothing have migrated into his closet, and I'm not sure if that is a good or bad thing. So, instead, I'm choosing not to think too much about. "You're welcome to join us."

"Is this the kind of scheme you three come up with when you're left to your own devices?"

I roll my eyes at him. "This is a *good* idea, Apollo. He has to go somewhere, so he might as well be with Rose. Because he's being evicted from my house."

"I get that." He sighs, pushing his hand through his hair, and then shrugs before reaching for his own jacket. "Okay, let's do this. I assume our first stop is the chapel to get him?"

"Yeah, I'm not excited about this part," I admit. "I really don't want to have to go down there again."

"I'll go with you, scaredy cat."

I stick my tongue out at him, but I don't decline his offer as we leave his house and make our way to the chapel.

"Sarah and Luna are meeting me here," I inform him as he parks in front of my place. "They want to be a part of the whole process, start to finish."

"Of course, they do," he mutters as I get out of his truck and hurry inside. "I guess I'll tell them that I was driving by and saw you, so I stopped, but we really need to tell them about us."

"I know." I worry my bottom lip as I unlock the front door and let us inside. "I know we do, and I agree, but today is not that day because we're moving a *body*."

"Soon. Very soon." After I've closed the door behind us, he cups my face in his warm hands and kisses me in that way that makes my toes curl and my stomach flutter. "Because I'm done being a secret."

"We're on the same page," I assure him as a car door slams outside. "They're here. Trust me, we'll get this done today, and then we'll set up a dinner or something for all six of us so we can tell them all at once."

"Okay." He nods once, seemingly placated for now, and I turn to open the door. Sarah and Luna are rushing up to the steps, with their men bringing up the rear, and I step back so they can all come in. "You brought the whole crew."

"If you think I'm going to miss this, you've lost your pretty little head," Wolfe says with a soft smile.

"Same goes," Tanner adds as they all file inside, and I close the door behind them. "Wow, June, this is incredible."

"Thanks." I follow their gaze and look around the space.

"It's starting to look like someone's house," Wolfe adds. "That kitchen is going to be awesome."

"I know, I can't wait to cook in it," I confess. "It's still a few months out from being finished, though."

I notice Apollo frowning in confusion.

"I thought you said you wanted to be in by the holidays," Tanner asks.

"You see how much needs to be done?" I sweep my arms wide, gesturing at everything that's not finished. "It's going to take more time. It's fine. Come on, let's get this over with."

I grab a cordless drill that we'll need when we get downstairs and then lead them through the future mudroom and down the stairs.

"It's creepy as fuck down here," Wolfe decides, making me laugh.

"Now you know what I'm dealing with." I grab the handle of the heavy door to the mausoleum. "Okay, so it's not necessarily scary in here, but it's a little alarming when you first see it. Luna, Sarah, and Apollo have seen it, but Wolfe and Tanner, consider yourself warned."

"Open her up," Tanner urges. "It'll be okay."

"You got permission for this?" Apollo asks me as I turn the knob.

"I filed the papers with the city. It's all taken care of." I pull the door open and feel inside for the light switch.

"Whoa," Tanner says, stepping inside.

"There's got to be a few hundred people down here." Wolfe follows behind his friend, saying, "It's really creepy that they're small squares and not regular sized."

"These are all cremated remains." I lead them down a row to where Daniel is. "Here he is."

"Daniel P. Snow," Luna reads, tracing the letters with her fingertips. "Wow, he was over eighty when he died."

"Let's get him out of here," I say and raise my drill.

"You know, there have to be ghosts down here," Wolfe says, and I whirl on him, shaking my finger at him. "Or not."

"Don't say that. I have to live here, you big jerk. There are no ghosts here."

"Nope. Not a one," he agrees. "Although, I live with Rose, and it's not so bad."

"No ghosts," I repeat before turning back to unscrew the front panel. "It's not even funny to suggest it."

"I wasn't being funny," Wolfe mutters as I pull out the first screw and then move on to the next. It doesn't take me more than five minutes to remove the front plate, and then I'm met with another one on the inside.

"I guess it's good that they reinforced these in case water ever got in here," I mutter as I start on plate number two.

"I'm going to keep this and use it as a marker for his grave until the new one is finished," Luna says behind me.

"Good idea," Sarah agrees.

"Okay, this one is off." Before I pull it away, I take a breath and look back at the five of them. "Why am I scared?"

"Because there are cremated remains in there?" Apollo asks, making me scowl. "Do you want me to do it?"

"No. I'll do it." I take another breath. "I need more light."

Suddenly, several phone flashlights shine over my shoulder, and I can see better.

I pull the plain panel away and find a simple, brown box with an engraved piece of brass that reads: *Daniel P. Snow.*

"This is him." I pull his box out and turn around toward the others. "I don't know why this feels a little anticlimactic, but I won't complain."

"Let's get him out of here," Luna suggests. "Do you want to replace that panel?"

"No, it's fine. They're all going to be removed eventually anyway. I want to get out of here."

It isn't until we're back outside that I take a deep sigh of relief.

"One down, a few hundred to go." I smile ruefully at the others. "We have to start somewhere, I guess."

"You guys can follow us up to the property. We already dug the hole, so it won't take long."

"You ride with me," Apollo says to me, and I nod, following him to the truck.

"She must be out of sorts if she didn't argue about riding with Apollo," I hear Sarah say to Tanner as they walk to their own vehicle.

"Yeah, we need to end the secrecy," I say to Apollo as I get into his truck.

"Is it weird that we're burying him to Rose's left when her husband is to her right?" I ask as we all stand around the gravesite.

"They need to be together," Luna reminds me.

"I know, it's just...weird." I shrug and gently lower the box containing Daniel's ashes into the small hole in the ground. "We should probably say something."

The others nod and look around at each other, no one volunteering.

"Okay, I'll do it." I blow out a breath. "We are respectfully laying the remains of Daniel P. Snow into his final resting place, here by the sea where he spent so much of his life and next to the woman he loved for his whole life. Due to unfortunate circumstances, Rose and Daniel couldn't be together in life, so we hope to reunite them in death. May they both rest in peace."

Wolfe shovels dirt over the box, and the others nod.

"Well done," Tanner says with a wink.

"I really do hope they both rest in peace," I reply, looking down at both graves. Luna places the panel from the mausoleum at the head of Daniel's grave, right next to Rose's.

"That's it," she says when the dirt is all filled in. "It's done. I'm glad they're finally together."

I sniff the air and smile when I smell the roses. "She's here."

"She's been here the whole time," Sarah says softly, tears in her blue eyes. "And I think she's happy."

"I hope so." I nod and reach for Sarah's hand as her other hand reaches for Luna's. For a long moment, we stand together, high on the cliffs with the sea wind blowing around us, waiting until the smell of roses fades away. "I really hope so."

April 8, 2000

Dear Diary,

You know, staying at Luna's is fun, but it also gets creepy sometimes. She has a GHOST living at her house! We've never actually seen her, but we smell her all the time. It smells like roses. Sometimes it's really strong, and other times it's faint. I stayed there last night, and we spent some time in our secret spot, up in the lighthouse. Sarah got to come for a while, too, but her mom made her go home after dinner.

I hate her mom.

Anyway, while we were up there reading a passage from the diary we found, we smelled the roses. The person who wrote the diary was named Rose, so we think it's Rose's ghost, trying to talk to us.

What does she want? We don't know. As long as she doesn't try to throw us down the lighthouse, or something, I guess it's not a big deal.

Grandma's house is really old, too. I don't think it's haunted, though. I'm sure we would have seen or heard or SMELLED something by now if it were.

Okay, I have to go eat dinner now.

XO,

June

Chapter Fourteen

Apollo

"Are we on for tonight?" I ask June as I press the phone to my ear with one hand and pull the door open with the other. It's early December, and it's damn cold outside, so I'm grateful for the heat that hits me when I walk inside.

"Yep," she says. "I'm going to call the girls today and find out when we can all get together for dinner. I think it's time you and I can come clean with everyone and stop hiding since I don't plan to stop having sex with you anytime soon."

That makes me grin. "Good, because I don't plan to stop either. Let me know what they say."

I walk into the living room of the house I've been working on for a few weeks, and my happiness turns to rage.

"Did you stop by the Thomas project yesterday?" I ask June, my voice calm.

"No, I haven't been by in a few days. In fact, no one

has because we're waiting on some special orders that Mrs. Thomas wants, so we're at a standstill. Are you over there?"

"Yeah." I sigh and prop my hands on my hips. I want to punch someone in the goddamn face. "You're going to want to come over here."

"What's wrong?" There's urgency in her voice now. "Your voice sounds weird. Tell me what's going on."

"Just come over. Trust me."

"Okay, I'll be there in ten."

She clicks off, and I blow out a breath. "Fuck."

I'd like to paint over the words on the wall and save her from seeing this, but she's the boss of this project, and she needs to be the one to decide how to proceed.

One thing that I've learned about June over the past couple of months is that she isn't as tough as she makes herself out to be, and she gets her feelings hurt like anyone else.

She just never lets anyone see it.

I think this is going to hurt her, and that pisses me off almost as much as the words on the wall.

I'm still staring at them when her car door slams outside, and I hurry back to the door so I can meet her.

"I don't even want to consider how fast you drove to get here so quickly," I say as I step outside and find her marching toward me.

"What's wrong?"

"Come on." I lead her inside, and when we get to the living room, she stops short.

"Holy shit. What in the actual fuck?"

Spray painted in bright red letters on the big wall of white drywall is: *FUCKING CUNT!*

"You've got to be kidding me," she mutters and rubs her eyes. "It's an easy fix, obviously. We haven't started to paint and texture yet, but for fuck's sake."

"Has anything else like this happened that you haven't told me about?" I ask her.

"Not like this, but"—she winces and refuses to look me in the eye—"I've had a few small things go missing."

"Why in the hell haven't you called the cops? Christ, Juniper, your *brother* is the cops. Call him."

"I figured it was Josh and asked Rob to keep an eye on him," she admits. "He's young and stupid, but this could ruin the rest of his life, and I was hoping that after he got the temper tantrum out of his system, he'd get bored and move on."

"Yeah, well, obviously, that's not the case. This is unacceptable."

She nods and pulls out her phone, dialing her brother and putting the call on speakerphone.

"Yo," Cullen says in greeting.

"Hey. I need you, if you're on duty."

"Tell me." His voice is hard and all business now.

"There's some vandalism at one of my job sites."

She gives him the address, and after he promises that he's on his way, she hangs up.

"I can't believe that pulling crap like this makes that kid happy," she says, pacing the floor. "It's stupid."

"People hold grudges, and sometimes, it keeps them

from thinking straight," I remind her. "You held a grudge against me for *years*."

"I never spray-painted *cunt* inside your house." She offers me a small grin. "Although, that probably would have been fun."

"You wouldn't do that."

She shrugs and returns to pacing. "Okay, I wouldn't. You're right, you can hold a grudge without being destructive."

Cullen walks inside and scowls when he sees the writing on the wall. "That's some creepy-ass serial-killer shit."

"Is that the professional word for it?" June asks, in full sassy mode. "Because I'd agree."

"Did you put up cameras like I told you to?" Cullen asks before walking through the house and checking the rooms to make sure nothing else has been messed with.

"That costs *money*, Cullen. Besides, we live in Huckleberry Bay, where this shit doesn't happen."

"Obviously, it does happen because I'm looking at it right now. I'm a cop, and I know exactly what happens in this town. Get yourself some goddamn cameras, Juniper."

"Fine." She sighs and closes her eyes. "Although, I don't need cameras for this. I know who it is."

"Who?"

"Josh, the young guy I had working for me for a while."

"Didn't you fire him more than a month ago?"

"I did." June swallows hard. "He's been causing little issues here and there, but nothing quite like this."

"And you're sure it's him?"

"I can't think of anyone else that would do this."

Cullen swears under his breath. "I'm going to throttle you. What kind of goddamn issues is that little son of a bitch causing? Better yet, why in the hell didn't you tell me?"

"I'm pretty sure he's stolen a few tools here and there and ruined a saw that I'd left on a site, but there hasn't been anything destructive like this."

"She was trying to be noble and keep him out of trouble," I add and raise an eyebrow, challenging her to argue. June only pins me with the look that says, *you're in so much trouble.*

"That's stupid," Cullen says to his sister.

"I thought he'd go away."

"And how is that working out for you?"

June gestures to the paint on the wall and sighs. "Not too well, if I'm being honest."

"I'd go find and arrest the little shit," Cullen says as he paces the floor. "But I need proof that he did this. Otherwise, it's hearsay, and the charge won't stick."

"Do you want fingerprints?"

"No, I wish you had put up cameras so would have video footage of him doing this."

"Fine," June mutters. "I'll install some today."

"Good." Cullen takes a few photos of the wall. "I'll take these to have on file, but you and Apollo should both file police reports anyway so we have documentation of it happening. Get me proof so I can lock him up, but be careful."

"I will."

Cullen looks over at me. "Keep her safe."

June's jaw drops. "He's not—"

"Oh, shut up," Cullen says, clearly irritated with his sister. "I'm not blind, am I?"

With that, he shakes his head and marches out the door.

"I guess we don't have to tell him." I turn back to her and see frustration all over her gorgeous face. "When do you want to go shopping for cameras?"

She scrubs her hands over her face and groans low in her throat.

If it wasn't mildly terrifying, it would be sexy as hell.

"I don't have time for this bullshit." She turns back to the red paint and fists her hands at her side. "I was *not* mean to that kid."

"You're right, you weren't mean, and you didn't do anything wrong. He just didn't like that you were his boss."

"Maybe, but I'm the one being punished. Now I'm really pissed. He wants to ruin a saw so I have to replace it? Fine. He wants to steal a drill or a nail gun here or there? I'll get over it. But *this*? This is such bullshit."

"I won't disagree with you." I step to her and drag my hand down her back. She leans her head on my shoulder. "Don't let it hurt your feelings, babe. He's a punk kid, and he'll be dealt with."

"Yeah. Okay, I'm over it." She sniffs, squares her shoulders, and firms her chin.

Then, just like that, she's done beating herself up.

"I'm going back to work," she says and pats my shoulder. "Have a good day."

"I think I need more than a shoulder pat."

Her eyes narrow. "No funny business on a—"

"Shut up." I grip her shirt in my fist and tug her to me, dropping my lips to hers. The kiss is long and slow, soothing us both, and when I pull back and smile down at her, she smiles back. "Have a nice day, dear. I'll see you tonight."

"Right." She swallows hard. "Tonight."

I nod and back away from her and toward the area of the house where I'm working, but she doesn't move for the door.

"June?"

"Yeah?"

"You're not working on this site today."

"Oh." She blinks, shakes her head, and laughs. "Right. See you."

She turns and walks out the door without looking back at the message on the wall, and I nod in satisfaction.

I did my job and distracted her.

"I WANT ICE CREAM," June announces as we walk out of Three Sisters Kitchen after having the best dinner I'd had in a long time.

"A minute ago, you said you were full."

"I am, but there's always room for ice cream. Besides, if we walk over to Huckleberry Delight, we'll get some of the food already in our stomachs to move down. It's a whole strategy."

"Your wish is my command." I take her hand in mine, threading our fingers, and we walk at a leisurely pace down the street toward the ice cream shop. "People we know saw us tonight."

"I know, but you know what? I don't care. We're having dinner with the others tomorrow night, and we'll spill the tea to them. I'm not going to hide anymore, Apollo."

"I think a few people were surprised." I shift to my left a bit, silently moving her so that she goes around some glass on the sidewalk instead of walking over it. "It's pretty well-known that we don't like each other."

"You know, I think it's good to keep people on their toes." June laughs a little. "Also, it's none of their business. I know they think it is because we live in a small town and they've known us all our lives, but it really isn't. I mean, my brother obviously figured it out, but it's none of the rest of the town's concern if they're not connected to us in a more personal way."

"No, it's not." Before we can walk into the shop, June's phone rings.

"Speaking of my brother," she mutters and answers, putting it on speaker. "Hey, what's up?"

"We arrested Josh today, not long after I left the crime scene, actually."

"What? How? All we have is hearsay, remember?"

"Yeah, well, he was pulled over for speeding, and he was completely shitfaced. So, he was arrested for DWI and underage intoxication, but we also found empty cans of red spray paint in his car. He was so fucking drunk that he laughed when we asked him about them. Then he admitted to the whole thing *after* his rights had been read to him, so it's admissible. He won't be bothering you anymore, sis."

"Good." June sighs in relief. "I'm glad that worked out, but I can't help but feel bad for him."

"He's not your responsibility," Cullen reminds her. "Have a good evening."

"You, too. Love you, bye."

"Love you, too."

She hangs up, and the smile she gives me is stunning. "This calls for *two* scoops of ice cream."

"I like the way you celebrate." I laugh, pulling open the door to Huckleberry Delight for her. Montana, the owner, is wielding an ice cream scoop and manning the counter, which is surprising.

"Hi, you two," she says, giving us a hesitant smile. "Are you hanging out together *voluntarily*? I didn't think you got along."

"Not everything stays the same," June says with a shrug.

"Okay, then. You have excellent timing because the rush just ended, and it's finally calm in here."

"I'm glad you stay busy because I don't know what I'd do if you ever went out of business," June says as she peers down into the glass-top freezer holding at least a dozen tubs of fresh ice cream.

"Don't even put that out into the universe," Montana

says with a cringe. "I plan to be here for a long, long time. So, what'll it be? I have some of the signature fall flavors left. Apple pie à la mode has been popular this season."

"I always get the same thing," June says with a grin. "Two scoops of the huckleberry ice cream in a dish with hot fudge drizzle."

"You got it." Montana turns to me with a smile. "And for you, Apollo?"

"I'll try that apple pie, please. Just one scoop in a waffle cone."

Montana is quick with that ice cream scoop and is passing our treats to us in no time.

"Anything else?"

"Not for me," June says, already digging in. "Oh, my god, Montana, you're a damn genius."

"Hey, could you write that down and leave the review online for me? That's one I'd like to print out and put on the wall." Montana winks as she passes me my change. "You two have a good night."

"Thanks."

We wave at her as we walk out of the shop, headed back to my truck parked at Three Sisters, but then June moves to a bench along the sidewalk and takes a seat.

"Let's eat this here and watch people walk by. I don't ever just sit in the middle of town and enjoy it, you know?"

"I guess I don't either." Sitting next to her, I kick my feet out and cross them at the ankles. "I wonder if anything's ever going to go in where the hardware store used to be."

I gesture with my chin to the empty storefront, and June nods.

"I heard that someone bought it, and they're splitting it into two sides. One side will be a clothing boutique, and the other is going to be a spa of some kind."

"Maybe when they open, you could go get a massage. Relax a little."

She snorts. "I don't like being touched that much, remember? So, having someone getting all handsy with me sounds like torture."

I look her up and down and then meet her gaze once more.

"You don't seem to mind when *I* get handsy."

"I'm getting used to it." She shrugs, finishes her ice cream, and tosses the empty cup into a nearby garbage can. "I definitely don't want strangers touching me like that. Ew. No. Gross."

I laugh as I toss my napkin into the trash and reach for June's hand. "Come on, let's go back to my place."

"Are you going to get handsy?" Her eyes are full of humor as I pull her to her feet.

"Hell yes, I'm going to get *very* handsy."

"Then lead on."

"It's getting so cold in the evenings." June dances back and forth beside me as I unlock the door, blowing on her hands to warm them up. "Winter is definitely almost here."

"It's not *that* cold out there. You were fine on the bench." I push the door open and let her walk in ahead of me.

"I know, but I'm suddenly *so cold.*" She shivers and heads straight for the couch to wrap herself up in one of the many throw blankets she's tossed about over the past few weeks. "Is the heat on in here?"

"Yes." I join her on the couch and pull her into my arms. "Come on, I'll share my body heat."

"It only helps if you're in the blanket." She hurries to shift the throw, covering us both and snuggling up next to me. "But this is *not* a cuddle session."

"Of course not. It's a warming-up session. Out of necessity."

"Exactly." She sighs as she wraps her arms around me and rests her head on my chest. "This is nice and warm."

"Good." I kiss the top of her head and breathe in the delicious scent of her hair. "Where do you get your red hair from?"

"No idea." She chuckles softly. "No one else in the family has it, so I assume my biological father or his family. It kind of reinforces the idea that Lauren, Cullen, and I have different fathers. We really don't look that much alike."

"I see a resemblance, but definitely not in your coloring." I kiss her hair again, and her hand starts to drift over my stomach and up my chest. "You must be warming up."

"Hmm." She shifts to straddle my lap so the blanket is around her back and she's resting her hands against the back of the couch. When she leans in to kiss me, it's not a soft kiss, but it's not hard and demanding either.

It's *familiar*. It's the kind of kiss that she gives because she knows me and is comfortable taking what she needs.

I fucking love that.

"Want you," she whispers, and between kisses, she crosses her arms in front of her, grabs the hem of her shirt, and pulls it over her head. She's wearing the hot-as-hell green bra that I love on her as much as I love it being on the floor with the rest of her clothes.

I sit up, wrap my arms around her, and unfasten the bra, and she lets it slide down her arms.

"I know this is going to sound sexist as fuck." I lean in and brush my nose across the tight nub of one nipple. "But I love your breasts."

"It's a hell of a lot better than hating them." She laughs and pushes her fingers into my hair as I kiss and lick her chest, her perfect breasts.

Suddenly, she stiffens, and my head whips up so I can look her in the face.

"What is it?"

She swallows hard. "I think I'm going to blow chunks."

"How romantic."

She tries to smile, but then she's scrambling off my lap and dashing to the bathroom. The door slams loudly behind her, and I'm left sitting on the couch, wondering what in the actual hell is happening.

Did she eat something that had spoiled at Three Sisters?

Something tells me that I wouldn't be at all welcome in the bathroom with her, so I grab her a glass of water and a cool washcloth before going to wait outside the bathroom door. I can hear her retching, and I feel bad for her.

With the water and cloth on standby, I hurry back to the bedroom and get some comfortable clothes ready for her, shifting my focus from sex to taking care of June while she works her way through whatever has decided to make her feel like shit.

Either way, I get to spend the night with her, and I consider that a win.

Chapter Fifteen

June

Did that really just happen?

Did I *really* just have to abandon Apollo's lap and all the seriously fun sexy time we were having to run—*half-naked*—through his house and lose all the delicious food I'd eaten this evening?

Leaning against the bathroom vanity, I stare at myself in the mirror. I look like I went a round with the champ, and it didn't go well for me at all. If I were the referee, I'd call it.

"What in the hell is going on with my stomach?" I whisper to my reflection. "If this is a virus, it's the weirdest virus I've ever had."

I brush my teeth and splash cold water over my face before I open the door and find Apollo standing on the other side, holding a glass of water and a washcloth.

"Thank you." I gratefully accept the water and take a long drink, relieved that my stomach has settled enough for it to stay down. "Sorry about that."

"Do you think you ate something bad?" He looks so concerned as he brushes a strand of my hair off my cheek. He's not even ogling my bare boobs, which is kind of sweet. "Because, if you did, we should let Mira know so she doesn't serve it to someone else."

"I don't know. My stomach has been off for a few days. It's probably an ulcer or a weird stomach condition because of stress. Or some kind of virus."

I feel my eyes widen as I stare at him.

"Shit, if it's a virus, I probably shouldn't be hanging out with you if I could be contagious."

"I'm good." He takes my hand and leads me to the bedroom. "I have a change of clothes here for you."

I love the way his muscles move and shift under his smooth skin, and without giving it another thought, I reach for him and pull him close.

"You know, I'm feeling a *lot* better now. We can pick up where we left off."

In fact, not only do I feel better, but also, I might spontaneously combust if he doesn't make love to me right this second.

I don't know if I've ever been this horny in my life.

"Honey, if you don't feel well, it's totally okay. I'm not mad or disappointed or anything."

"I will be if you don't jump my bones." I shed my pants, move to the bed naked as the day I was born, and crook my finger in invitation. "Come here, Winchester."

"How do you go from heaving to sexy in less than ten minutes?" He may be hesitant, but he's not arguing as he strips out of his clothes and joins me in bed.

"Whatever it was, it's passed, and now, I want you even more than I did earlier."

His cock hardens in my hand as I stroke him and kiss my way down his torso until I'm wrapping my lips around him.

"Holy shit." His hands dive into my hair and hold on as I work him over nice and easy at first, and then I take him deeper until he's panting and fisting my hair so hard my follicles hurt in the best kind of way. "Need you."

He sits up, takes my face in his hands, and kisses me hard as he flips us so I'm tucked beneath him and he's kneeling between my legs.

"Now." I reach down and rub myself, unable to quench this crazy thirst that's clawing at me. "Now, now, now."

He pushes into me, and we both moan in pleasure.

"Hard," I demand, lifting my hips in a desperate invitation, which he happily accepts.

"Jesus," he mutters. "I fucking love everything about you."

Yeah, the sex is *damn* good. It's always been out of this world with Apollo, which really pissed me off at first.

Now, I can't get enough of him.

That should also piss me off, but it doesn't because I've gone and fallen in love with the big jerk.

Except, he isn't a jerk at all.

He's maybe one of the nicest people I know, and that's been a huge adjustment for me, as well.

Picturing my life without him, going back to the way

it was before we started this wild affair, makes me so sad that I can't even contemplate it.

It's not an option for me now, which scares the absolute hell out of me. This man has the power to completely devastate me, and he doesn't even know it.

I'm in no hurry to tell him either.

"Look at me." His voice is rough and hard, and my eyes snap open. "I want you to fucking *come*, and I want you to say my name when you do."

"That's cheesy."

He takes my chin in his hand, and his eyes are so fucking intense, it makes everything in me tense.

"God, you're sexy," I mutter as I feel the orgasm grow.

"Do it," he says, pounding even harder, and I fall apart. Apollo's name falls from my lips as wave after wave of sensation rolls through me.

He groans and follows me over, and then he rolls to the side and tugs me tight against his chest.

"So, getting sick makes you horny." He swallows hard as he catches his breath. "Good to know."

I smile. "I guess so. This isn't after-sex cuddles."

His hand drifts up and down my back, making me want to stretch into his touch and purr like a kitten.

"Of course not." He kisses my forehead. "Do you need anything?"

"I think I'm kind of sleepy now."

"Makes sense to me. You've had a busy time of it tonight. Drift off, babe. I'm right here with you."

I can't keep my eyes open, so I do as he says. I relax and let sleep take over.

I CAN'T BELIEVE Apollo talked me into staying home today.

I *own* the company. Sick days aren't a luxury that I can indulge in. Sure, I have an excellent crew, but I need to be out in the field every day, checking on job sites. He even asked me not to go to the chapel, which I almost threw down about before I ended up having to run to the bathroom.

There may not be a chance in hell of finishing it by Christmas, but that doesn't mean that I can't work on it anyway. Speaking of Christmas, it's right around the corner, and I haven't done any shopping, which means I have way too much to do to just lie around Apollo's house all day.

I will admit, though, it felt good to sleep in a bit. Whatever's decided to piss off my stomach has made me so freaking *sleepy*. I'm so over it, and if I'm not better in a couple of days, I'll have to break down and go to the doctor, which I *hate*. So, here's to hoping this passes and I start to feel better on my own.

Ignoring my rolling stomach, I get dressed, pull on my sturdy coveralls and work boots, and then pile my hair under my old, beat-up trucker hat so it stays out of my way.

Happy with that result, I set off for the chapel so I

can take a look around before I head to the job sites and check in with my guys there.

Admittedly, they likely have everything under control, but I like to touch base with them in case they have questions or any issues.

When I pull up to the chapel, I immediately scowl at the number of trucks parked out front. Before I even make it to the front door, I can hear power tools and talking inside. Someone has a radio playing.

Stopping in the doorway as I let my eyes adjust, I feel like I've been hit in the solar plexus. My walls are being textured. The kitchen cabinets are being painted, and Apollo is giving instructions for how the light fixtures are supposed to be installed.

There have to be twenty men in here, bustling about as if this is the most important project in town. There are certainly more workers here than what I have on staff. Even my brother has a tool belt slung around his waist and is carrying trim in and out of one of the bedrooms.

"What's happening?" I ask.

Apollo's head whips around, and when he sees me, he grins, but then his smile drops into a concerned frown as he climbs off his ladder and hurries over to me.

"I thought you said you were going to take a sick day," he says as he reaches me.

"No, *you* said that. What in the hell is happening here? I didn't hire them to do this."

"I know." He glances back at them and then turns to me with a very satisfied grin. "It was supposed to be a surprise, but you're not good at taking directions. Are you feeling okay?"

Right now, something's doing the rumba in my stomach, but I shrug. "I'm fine. Talk to me, Apollo."

"Okay, so when you said the other day that you wouldn't be able to move in here before the holidays like you wanted, it got me to thinking. You obviously didn't ask your staff to help you, even though you promised you would."

"I didn't—"

"So, I made some calls, and everyone agreed that they'd take today to get ahead of things, and then, schedules willing, they'll be here from three until six in the afternoon every day until it's done. They can spare those hours around all the other projects they're working on."

"I don't employ all of these people."

"No, but they all *know* you and care about you. Juniper, we live in a small, tight-knit community. They want to help, so they are."

"Christmas is only two weeks away."

"Well, then, we'd better get crackin'."

I blow out a breath, feeling perilously close to tears. "This is too much."

"No, it's not. No one feels that way at all. You've put this project off for *months,* letting it take the back seat to literally everyone else as you work your ass off for them. This is your home, June, and we all want you to be able to live in it as soon as possible. It'll take a load off your plate."

"I mean, it will do that." It's tough to admit, but he's

not wrong. "It'll help my stress level a lot. Maybe that's why my stomach's been off."

"It could absolutely be the case. Let us do this for you, Juniper. We *want* to help you."

"Am I allowed to jump in, too?"

"It's your house, so of course you can—just not today. Today, I want you to go back to my place or to your grandma's and relax. Hell, even the inn would work, but I want you to take it easy until you're feeling better. You need the rest."

"You're so damn bossy. If I had known how bossy you are, I'm not sure that I'd be letting you do things to me all the time."

He smirks and leans in to whisper in my ear. "You didn't mind my bossiness last night."

"That was different." I laugh and then look around at all guys working in the chapel, feeling so much gratitude and love that I don't even know what to do with myself. "You've already done so much in here."

"We're hoping to make a lot of progress today," he agrees. "You already had all the fixtures and materials stored in your guest bedroom, so we're installing them. If there's anything that we do wrong, tell us and we'll fix it."

"Thank you." I want to kiss the hell out of him, but the thought of doing that in front of all of these people is absolutely mortifying, so I just smile. "I mean it."

"You're welcome." He winks at me, and my chest squeezes.

Damn, I have it bad for this man.

"Now, get out of here and rest. Don't make me sic my

sister on you."

"Okay, okay." I turn to walk out the door, but then turn back to him. "Can I sit in there and supervise? I won't get up. You won't even know that I'm here."

He raises an eyebrow, and I narrow my eyes at him.

"Fine. Keep all the fun for yourself, then." He laughs at my back as I walk away.

"Have a good rest," is all he says as he firmly shuts the door behind me, closing me out of my own goddamn house.

"Well, how do you like that," I mutter as I shuffle over to my truck. I admit, I'm already sleepy again, and that irritates me. "I just got kicked out of my own house."

I guess a nap doesn't sound too bad, but rather than go back to Apollo's place, I head for my grandma's house.

I haven't checked in on her in a few days, and I miss her.

Only, when I get there, she's not home.

"What a weird day," I mutter as I pad my way up the stairs to my childhood bedroom. My phone pings with a text from Luna.

LUNA: *Rumor has it that you're not feeling well today.*

"Jesus, does the entire town know? Why didn't he just take out an ad in the paper?" Chalking the irritation up to fatigue, I reply to her.

Me: Yeah, not great. Came to Grandma's to nap for a while.

Luna: Okay, get some rest and feel better!

After setting my phone to silent, I slide into the old familiar bed and almost instantly fall asleep.

———————

"DON'T WAKE HER UP."

It's a loud whisper that I assume is meant to be quiet but definitely is *not* quiet.

"We need to talk to her." Another whisper.

"She needs sleep *more*."

"I'm awake." I sit up and scrub my hands down my face. When I crack my eyes open, I find my two best friends standing beside my bed, both peering down at me with concern. "Hi."

"Hey. We didn't know if we should wake you," Luna admits as she reaches over and presses the back of her hand to my forehead, which I immediately bat away. "I want to see if you have a fever."

"I don't." I glance to the window and frown. "What time is it?"

"It's after five," Sarah says and sits at the foot of my bed.

"Holy shit, I slept the whole day away." I scowl and stretch my arms over my head. "I hate it when I do that."

"I'm sorry that you're not feeling well," Luna says and sets a basket on my bed. "We brought you a whole bunch of stuff to help settle your stomach. Ginger tea, saltines, Sprite, broth...there's a lot in here."

"Thanks." I grab a pack of saltines, rip open the clear package, and stuff one in my mouth. "I'm really hungry."

"I'm surprised you're here and not over at Apollo's," Sarah says, trying to act casual.

"Why would I be over there?"

"Oh, come on," Luna says, rolling her eyes. "We're not stupid, June. We've seen you two together a hundred times since before Halloween, and it's obvious to anyone with eyes that you're together. Stop pretending that you aren't."

I lower the cracker to my lap and stare down at it. "I don't know why we kept it a secret. Well, yeah, actually, I do. It was because I told him that I wanted to because, what if we just slept together a few times and then it was over, you know? There was no need to announce that to the world."

"But it hasn't been just a few times," Sarah says softly.

"No, and I don't think we'll stop any time soon. We were going to tell everyone this week, but then I wasn't feeling well, and it seems like there's been something constantly keeping us from telling you. Frankly, I feel a little guilty that I'm talking to you about this because Apollo and I agreed that we'd tell everyone together, but holy shit, it feels so good to get this off my chest."

"I admit, my feelings were hurt at first," Luna says. "Him not telling me, I understand, but you're my best friend, and you kept me out. After I thought about it for a bit, I realized that it's not about me. I'm so glad you're together. Given how explosive you are when you can't stand each other, I bet it's like a nuclear bomb when you *do* like each other."

"It's pretty wild," I agree, nodding. "Now, if I could shake this stomach thing, everything would be great. I need to get to work, and Christmas is a couple of weeks away. I have shit to do."

Luna and Sarah share a look, and then their gazes return to me.

"What?"

"Well, we brought you something else," Luna says, reaching for her handbag. She pulls out a slender box that is very clearly marked as a pregnancy test.

"Whoa." I hold my hands up in defense. "Let's not go overboard. It's a queasy stomach, that's all."

"Honey, how long have you been sleeping with Apollo?" Sarah asks.

I sigh and think back. "I don't know, since before Halloween. Maybe a week or two before that."

"You need to take this test." Luna holds it out to me, but I cringe away from it.

"I'm *not* pregnant."

"Great. You can go pee on this, get a negative result, and then we can take you to the doctor to figure out what's up with your stomach. Win-win. Now, go pee."

"You and your brother are both really bossy."

"Yep." She smiles serenely, not backing down, so I grab the box out of her hand and stomp into the bathroom.

"I'm not fucking pregnant," I mutter as I open the box and quickly read the instructions. Just pee on the thingy and wait a few minutes.

Fine. I can do that.

When I'm done, I return the stick to its little foil packaging, return to my room, and drop the stick onto the bed.

"We can check it in a few minutes."

"Great, thanks." Luna pats the bed. "Sit. You look exhausted."

"I'm probably dehydrated." I blow out a breath, suddenly nervous. "I'm not drinking enough water. That's what it is, I'm sure."

"That could be," Sarah agrees, but it's clear they both think I'm full of shit.

And until right this minute, it never occurred to me that I could be *with child*, as Annabelle would say.

"We've been careful," I insist, answering a question that no one asked. "I'm on the fucking pill, and most of the time, we use condoms, too. Not every time, but a lot of the time. Like, at least half."

I blow out a breath because I'm rambling and need to stop.

"Shit, we haven't used condoms in a really long time. Still, I take my pill every day without fail."

"Then maybe you're not pregnant," Luna says as she reaches for the stick in the package. "You want to look, or do you want me to?"

"You do it." I stand and walk to the window, chewing on my thumbnail. Damn it, I can't be pregnant.

I. Can't.

His reaction when he realized he didn't wear a condom that first time was intense, and he was so freaked out that it took him an hour to calm down.

Jesus, I assured him that we couldn't get pregnant because I was on the pill.

"Uh, June?"

I close my eyes and then turn back to them.

"Yeah?"

"Open your eyes."

"I don't want to."

"June," Sarah says. "It's okay."

"I'm not pregnant?" My eyes pop open in relief, but when I see their faces, I know I'm wrong.

"No, you *are* pregnant," Luna says. "She means that everything's going to be okay."

"Holy shit, I'm going to throw up."

I run back into the bathroom and drop to my knees by the toilet in time to get violently sick. Someone's rubbing my back, and someone else is holding a wet cloth to the back of my neck.

"I don't like to be touched," I mutter between bouts of vomiting, but they don't stop.

When I've lost everything I've ever eaten in my life, I sit back on my heels and take the wet cloth, rub it over my face, and then turn to rest my head on Sarah's shoulder.

"What am I going to do?"

"You're going to come back into your bedroom and eat a cracker," Luna responds.

"I'll go heat up some water for tea," Sarah says when we reach my room. She hurries off, and I sit on the side of the bed.

"At least this explains all the throwing up and being so tired."

"Yeah, well, I think I'd rather have the flu."

"I know." She sits beside me and wraps her arm around my shoulders. "If you don't want this baby, you have options."

That brings tears to my eyes. "It's not that I *don't* want this baby, it's that I didn't think I wanted *any* babies at all. I thought you and Sarah would have a dozen kids between you, and I'd be the cool aunt who gives out gum and ice cream like it's going out of style."

"I'll invest in a good dentist," Luna says dryly.

"I have hot water," Sarah announces, carrying a tray with a steaming mug and a plastic bear holding honey. "Annabelle says that she'll check in on you in a little while."

"Did you tell her?"

She looks at me like I'm crazy and slowly shakes her head. "No, she only knows that you don't feel well. Jesus, June, this is your news to tell, not mine."

"I'm sorry." I gratefully accept the mug and blow on the hot steam. "I know you wouldn't tell her. I'm panicking and don't know how Apollo will react to this. Maybe I shouldn't tell him."

They stare at me and then burst into laughter.

"This isn't funny."

"You'll have to tell my brother sooner or later because, at some point, you won't be able to hide it. Besides, he helped create this little bundle of joy. He should know."

"What if he gets mad and, like, punches holes in the

walls or throws a fit and then he leaves and I never see him again?"

I'm met with silence.

"Who did that to you?" Luna wants to know.

"My mom." I shrug and sip the still-hot tea. "Guys, in my experience, children aren't a great thing to have around. They don't bring joy. They bring stress and inconvenience. Even after my mom left us with Grandma, that's what we were for her, as well. Sure, she wasn't a jerk about it, but I knew that it wasn't fun for her. I don't want to bring a kid into that."

"I'm so sorry."

We all turn toward the doorway, finding my sweet little grandma standing there with tears in her eyes and her hands clasped at her waist.

"Oh, shit, you weren't supposed to hear that."

"I beg to differ," she says as she steps into the room. "I'm sorry that you felt that way as a child. You three *did* overwhelm me, but I never meant for you to feel as if you were an inconvenience. It's just that I raised my girl, but I didn't expect to have to raise my grandbabies, as well. I don't mean that as horribly as it sounds."

"I know you didn't."

"You three brought me *so much* joy, Juniper Snow. You make me laugh, and you make me proud. Sometimes, you make me want to twist your ear off because you frustrate me, which is entirely normal, but I feel that way *because* I love you, not instead of. Someday, you'll feel the same way about your own children."

So, she didn't hear the part about my being pregnant.

That's a relief.

"I'm sure I will, Grandma. I'm fine, honest."

She kisses my forehead and then walks out of the room, closing the door behind her.

"Your mom sounds as lovely as my parents were." Sarah's voice is as dry as paper. "At the end of the day, you have to remember that you aren't her any more than I am the assholes who don't deserve to be called my parents. You'll make your family the way you want it to be, and I personally think that you'll be a great mom."

"It's too soon," I whisper. "We haven't even used the L word."

"The way you wrinkle your nose at the idea is inspiring," Luna says with a laugh.

"I know you," Sarah adds, pointing her perfectly manicured finger at me. "And I know that if you didn't love Apollo, you wouldn't be sleeping with him. You wouldn't be spending so much time with him because you don't waste your time on people who don't matter to you."

"Yeah, well, it's the early days. Sure, I care about him, and he admitted last night that he loves the sexy time, but that's not necessarily a declaration of love."

"It's a start, and until you actually tell him what's going on so you both have all the information, you can't move forward in any way." Luna's chin firms as she continues to lecture me. "This is something you need to work out together."

"You would make a really great psychologist."

She stares at me until I huff out a breath.

"Fine, but give me a few days to wrap my head around this and decide how I want to tell him and how I want to move forward."

"I think that's fair," Sarah says and shrugs when Luna turns to her. "What? It *is* fair, Luna. I know he's your brother, but this isn't about you, and it's a lot of information for June to process. She needs to clear her head before she unloads on Apollo."

"Exactly." I nod in agreement. "That's all it is, clearing my head before I tell him, and then he and I will come up with a plan together."

"Don't put it off too long," Luna suggests. "It'll only get harder, and then he'll wonder why you didn't tell him sooner, which will be one more thing to argue about."

"Right." I bite my lip. "Okay, I'll tell him in a day or two, tops."

"In the meantime," Sarah adds, "what do you need?"

"I really want some chocolate cake right now."

"You should say the baby wants it," Luna says. "Then the calories don't count."

"Holy shit." I swallow hard before flinging myself back on the bed and covering my face with a pillow.

"Don't smother yourself." Sarah takes the pillow off my face.

"I'm having a *baby*. How in the hell did this happen?"

"You don't know?" Luna asks.

"Don't make me hurt you."

May 23, 2009

Dear Diary,

I lost my virginity. It sucked. The end.
XO,
June

Chapter Sixteen

Apollo

"Hey, it's June." It makes me smile that she starts her voice mail by saying it's her, as if I don't have caller ID. "Just letting you know that I won't be over tonight. I'm going to hang with Grandma for a few days. She's been lonely. See you later."

I frown, listen to the message again, and then toss my phone aside.

It's been three days since I've seen June outside of work, and it looks like it's going to stay that way for a little while. She's been distant, and if I didn't know any better, I'd say she's actually trying to avoid me, but I have no idea why.

When I do see her at work, she doesn't meet my eyes and barely speaks to me. There are no coy looks, no flirtations, and absolutely zero stolen touches.

My phone rings, and I grab it, hoping it's June, but it's Wolfe.

"Whatcha doing?" he asks.

"Nothing. Just got home from work. What's up?"

"I thought I'd invite some guys over to the barndo-minium tonight. We can shoot some pool and have some beers and stuff."

"Will there be food?"

"Of course, there will be food. All-you-can-eat pizza."

"Let's do it. When?"

"Come over now."

"See you in a few."

I cut off the call and grab my keys and wallet, deciding that hanging out with the guys will at least stop me from doing something stupid like chasing down June.

Wolfe's family has always owned the property next to my family's, and after his parents passed away, he inher-ited it. He tore down the old house and built a freaking sweet garage in the style of a barndominium, which seems to be all the rustic rage these days. The garage has ten bays—one for each of Wolfe's fancy cars with the others housing the cars he's working on but won't take to his commercial garage in town.

After he moved in with my sister at the lighthouse, he converted the loft above the garage into a sort of man cave. There are pool and air hockey tables, a flat screen spot to watch the games, and a full bar. It's become our official hangout spot when we want to get away from the girls.

Luna made a joke about hanging a *Boys Only* sign on the door, so he did. She rolled her eyes when she saw it, but I know that she thought it was funny.

The bays are closed when I pull up, so I park next to Tanner's SUV, head inside without knocking, and walk straight up the stairs that lead to the converted loft.

"Hey," Wolfe says with a grin. "Tanner just arrived with the pizza."

"Nice. I love it when I have good timing."

"Are you up here?" Zeke calls out below.

"Follow the scent of pizza," Tanner suggests, and I'm surprised to see Indigo Lovejoy walk in behind Zeke.

"I brought a friend. He deserves beer and pizza after everything that I put him through."

"I've had worse," Indigo replies with a grin, and reaches for the offered beer Tanner holds out to him. "But I won't pass this up."

"Welcome," Wolfe says and gestures to the food and the whole space. "Make yourself at home. Cullen and Scott are coming over, too."

"What's the occasion?" I tip my bottle up and take a sip of beer. "This is a bona fide party."

"Bachelor party," Wolfe admits with a grin. "Luna and I decided we're sick of waiting for a good time to get married, and we're going to do it during the Christmas party at the inn next week."

The room goes quiet. My jaw drops. Then we're all congratulating him at once.

"Luna is still getting her big wedding," he continues. "Most of the town plans to be there anyway, and her parents will still be in town."

"They get here tomorrow," I confirm. "I spoke with Dad today. They're excited to stay at the inn."

"Luna's so fucking nervous. She wants them to love it. I told her it's going to be great and there's nothing to worry about, but she doesn't listen to me."

"She never has," I reply with a chuckle. "That's awesome. I'm excited for you guys."

"What about you and Sarah?" Indigo asks, turning to Tanner. "You set a date yet?"

"Sometime next summer," Tanner replies as we hear more voices on the stairs. "I'll help where she wants me to, but for the most part, I'm leaving it all up to her. This is her vision, and I'm happy to let her have it."

"Smart man," Indigo replies with a laugh. "Hey, Cullen. Scott."

"Were you just talking about my sister?" Scott asks. "She's already asked me to give her away at your wedding, so I think she's planning more than you realize."

"Of course, she is," Tanner says with a smile. "Must be a woman thing."

After Cullen puts the beer he brought into the fridge, he grabs a slice of pizza, joining the party.

"So what happened today?" I ask Zeke as we wander over to the pool table. When he stares at me blankly, I clarify, "With you and Indigo. You said you felt sorry for him."

"Oh, that." Zeke laughs and bites into his slice. "I need him to find me a new place to live, and I'm fucking picky."

"I've dealt with worse," Indigo says again.

"Why are you moving?" Scott wants to know. "Those condos you live in are *sick*."

"Yeah, I know, but my neighbor is a goddamn pain in my ass. It's time I move before I kill her and spend the rest of my life in jail."

"Don't say shit like that," Cullen says. "You know I'm a cop."

"I'm not doing it, am I?" Zeke blows out a breath.

"The problem is that everything for sale around here is a single-family home, and he doesn't want that. He wants another condo with a water view, and there aren't any available that aren't already in his current building."

"Told you"—Zeke points his pizza at Indigo—"I don't want to have to deal with the upkeep of a house. The condo is perfect."

"Maybe, and I'm going out on a limb here," Wolfe says, holding up his hands, "you should kiss and make up with Cherry Dubois so you can stay in your perfect condo. Stop being a stubborn ass about it."

"It's Cherry Dubois?" Scott frowns over at Zeke and turns his hat backward before he racks the pool balls. "Not only is she really nice, but she's also hot. I've been thinking about asking her out on a date, but my work schedule at the fire hall has been stupidly busy lately, so I haven't had a chance."

Zeke's eyes narrow on Scott, and I grin. "You like her."

"Bullshit, asshole," Zeke says, but I keep grinning, not at all offended.

"You do, but you don't want to."

"I don't usually go for the annoyingly bossy type,"

241

Zeke reminds me. "Let's change the subject. What about you and June?"

"What about me and June?"

Cullen's eyes cut to me as he chalks the end of a pool cue.

"You've been all over town together the past few months, looking mighty cozy together."

"Cozy? Who the hell uses the word *cozy*?" Indigo asks.

"He knows what I'm talking about," Zeke says, still watching me.

"Do you have a problem with me, Zeke?"

"I never have before," the other man admits. "I actually like you a lot. But it pisses me off when a man is with a woman but won't admit it to anyone because they're embarrassed of said woman."

"Who the fuck said I was embarrassed of June?" I set my bottle down. "You don't know anything about it."

"That's my point. No one does," he agrees. "So, what is it? Are you fucking around with her just for the sex, or is there something there? Because I *like* June, and she doesn't deserve that bullshit."

I push my hand through my hair and turn away. I want to kick his ass, but he's looking out for the woman I love, so I have to respect that.

"Is that what everyone thinks?" I look from man to man, staring them in the eyes. "That I'm just fucking around with her? That I'm embarrassed of her?"

"You've been seen out on dates or riding around together," Wolfe says, his voice level and calm. "You used to despise each other, and now you're together a lot, man. This is a small town, and people talk. If you and June aren't setting the narrative straight, then everyone else will write the story for you."

"Motherfucker." I pace the length of the loft, frustration rolling through me. I promised June that we'd tell our friends together, but damn it, I'm so fucking sick of hiding that I don't give a shit anymore. I'll beg for forgiveness later. "Yeah, okay."

I rub my hand down my face and turn back to the now-quiet room.

"We're together—not just *fucking*." I glare at Zeke, who's crossed his arms over his chest. "Sure, there's sex, but it's more than that."

"Keep talking," Cullen advises.

"She's so stubborn that, if I didn't love her so much, I'd want to strangle her. She's funny as hell, fun to be with, and so damn sweet when she wants to be. She might seem like a hard ass, and she can be, for sure, but she's a softie. I sound like an idiot."

"No, you don't." Wolfe shakes his head. "Keep going."

"We've been together for a few months. She wanted to keep it quiet because, well, she has baggage, I guess. I think that, if it didn't work out, she didn't want to have to explain that to everyone."

"Is it not going to work out?" Tanner inquires.

"If I have anything to say about it, it'll stick for the rest of my life. This is Juniper Snow we're talking about, and she doesn't take orders from anyone, not even me. I don't want anyone to think that what I have with June is insignificant or something I'm ashamed of because that couldn't be further from the truth. I mean, just look at her. She's gorgeous and successful and—"

I sigh, rest my hands on my hips, and look at my shoes as I try to pull my thoughts together.

"I love her," I admit. "You can razz me all you want for that, but it's true. So, yeah, fuck that embarrassment nonsense."

Zeke grins and holds his hands up in surrender when I pin him with my glare. "Just checking, man."

"You egged me on purposefully."

"Hell yes, I did."

"Way to go, Nosy Nancy," Indigo says, fist-bumping Zeke.

"Do me a solid and keep this here for now." I rub my hand over my mouth, thinking about how distant June's been over the past few days. "Not because she's a fucking secret, but because she didn't want to advertise it yet."

"We won't, but don't you dare tell Luna I knew before she did."

"Sarah either," Tanner adds.

"Deal. Okay, let's talk about someone else's love life. Indigo?"

"Not me." The other man laughs and shakes his head. "I just broke it off with someone, so I'm as single as they come, and that's perfectly fine with me."

"Women are overrated," Zeke says before backtracking. "Well, some are."

"Let's play pool," Scott suggests, gesturing to the table. "And drink. Is this a bachelor party, or what?"

"Yeah, focus," Tanner says with a laugh. "Let's do this."

———

"Where are you today?" I frown when June doesn't immediately answer me. I'm not a controlling person, but it's been a fucking week, and I miss her.

"I'm out and about," she says.

"How are you feeling? Is your stomach better?"

"I—" She pauses, and I scowl at the screwdriver I'm holding. "I'm doing better."

"Juniper."

"I am. Really. I'm helping Luna at the inn today. There's so much left to do now that a Christmas party has turned into a wedding, as well. Why? Where are *you*?"

"At your chapel, and when you weren't here, it made me worry."

Her voice softens. "Sorry. I don't know when I'll be over there again. Actually, you know what? That's not true. The bodies in the basement get to be moved in two days."

"*Two* days?"

"Yeah, the city called and told me the found time to move them to the cemetery. So, I'll definitely be there for that. Anyway, I don't know when I'll see you."

"June, why do I get the feeling that you're avoiding me?"

245

"Don't be ridiculous."

"I'm coming to the inn."

"No!" I hear her footsteps as she paces. "I mean, you don't have to do that."

"My parents are there, and I've hardly seen them since they arrived yesterday. I'm coming over right now."

I hang up before she can argue with me and stow my tools in the mudroom before heading to my truck.

I'm sick and tired of June avoiding me, but I wasn't lying when I told her I haven't seen my parents much since they got to town. We were supposed to all have dinner last night, but I ended up working late on a project across town, so I couldn't make it.

It's been a cold week in Huckleberry Bay. The town decorations are all up, and the garland and lights make everything feel festive as I drive toward the lighthouse.

When I pull to a stop in front of the inn, I whistle long and slow. "Holy shit. The elves have been damn busy."

Red bows and garland are draped across the front of the building. The old Ford that we found in the barn and had restored is parked under the portico, a small wreath hanging on the grill. It looks like something off a postcard.

Once I walk inside, I find several tall Christmas trees, fully decorated with thousands of ornaments, and lanterns sit on each step leading up the staircase.

"Did Sarah paint this?" I ask Luna as she walks in from the kitchen. She looks up at the painting I'm pointing at. It's of the inn decorated for the holidays, and Luna lights up with pride and happiness.

"Yes, isn't it perfect for the holidays?"

"It's beautiful," I confirm. "How's it going in here?"

"Better than I expected, actually. Mom and Dad have been a huge help. We're right on track with everything. What are you up to?"

"I came to see Mom and Dad and to check in with June."

"Why would you need to check in with June?" she asks.

Well, no better time than the present, I guess. "Because she and I are...together."

Her eyebrows climb, but she doesn't look shocked.

"And you already knew that."

"I kind of figured it out. I love it, by the way. My best friend and my brother? Hell yes."

"Where is she?"

"Oh, she just left. Said she had some errand to run or something."

I huff out a breath and rake a hand through my hair.

"Did you give her a heads-up that you were headed this way?"

"Unfortunately. She's been avoiding me, and I'm ready to shake some sense into her."

"I think she's been really busy, Apollo. Honest." She bites her lip, and before I can ask any questions, my dad walks into the room.

"Luna, I love these old lighthouse magazines that you have sitting out in the library. They're fascinating—oh, hi, son. Come on in and sit with me in the library."

"You know what? I think I will. Where can I find a cup of coffee?"

"There's some on the sideboard in the dining room." Luna gestures to her right. "There are muffins and scones in there, too. Help yourself."

I do just that. Armed with fresh coffee and sugar, I follow my dad into the library, which has an incredible view of the ocean. We sit in the leather chairs that face the floor-to-ceiling window, giving us an unblocked view of the waves below.

"How do you feel after your trip yesterday?" I bite into a scone and glance at Dad, who's watching me with a big grin on his face. "What?"

"You look frustrated. It must be a woman."

"I—" I laugh and take another bite of scone. "Yeah, I'm frustrated over a woman."

"They're clever beings, aren't they?"

"I was thinking more like irritating."

He looks over his shoulder as if to make sure my mom isn't standing right behind him, and then he leans closer to me. "Sometimes that's the case, yes. Want to talk about it?"

"I feel like all I do is talk about it." I blow out a breath before taking a sip of coffee. "Juniper Snow."

"Really?" He raises an eyebrow in surprise. "I wasn't expecting that."

"Why?"

"Well, because you were always sniping at each other. I didn't think you liked each other."

"We've smoothed all of that out."

"About time. I've always liked that girl. She's damn talented, too."

"I know. She's remodeling that little white chapel in town. She's going to live in it."

"Is that right? I can see her doing something like that. Good for her."

"She's avoiding me." I don't like saying that out loud. "I'm sure I did something to piss her off, but I have no idea what, and she won't talk to me about it."

"Ah, the old cold shoulder." He nods as if he knows all about that. "It happens from time to time. It's been my experience that, if I give your mom some space and let her work through the mad, she'll come out the other side and let me have it. Then I apologize, and we get on with our wonderful life."

"She's had a damn week."

He taps his fingers on the arm of the chair, which is something he only does when he's concerned. "That's quite a mad she's in."

"And I don't know why."

"That is irritating, but you'll figure it out. My son isn't an idiot."

"I feel like one today."

"Nah." He reaches over and pats my shoulder. "How's the electrical business?"

"Busy."

"And everything else?"

I'm quiet for a moment as I watch the waves crash against the cliffs. The ocean looks angry today.

"As soon as I figure out what makes Juniper happy, everything will be just about perfect."

"Good for you, son." He settles deeper into the chair and sighs with contentment. "You're happy. Luna's getting married and built this amazing new business while still managing to take care of the light. My kids are the coolest people I know."

I glance over and find him smiling at me.

"We really are pretty cool, aren't we?"

"Damn right."

Chapter Seventeen

June

"Who thought it would be a good idea to throw this party right between Christmas and New Year's?" I blow some hair out of my eyes and take a breath. "Hanging all of these lights is a lot of work, but it's going to look awesome."

"That's the last strand," Luna assures me. "I'm sorry that I keep adding things. I know it's a pain in the butt, but it's not *only* a huge holiday party. I wanted to throw the party after Christmas day so more people could come. I didn't want anyone to feel like they had to choose between spending time with their own families and coming out to see the inn."

"It's not a pain in the butt at all, and you should have the wedding you want. Besides, I don't mind doing it. It's all good."

"I think the timing is great," Sarah says as she steps

off a ladder. "And speaking of timing, June, have you taken the time to talk to Apollo?"

I scowl at her. "We don't want to talk about that."

"Yeah, I think we do," Luna adds. "But I take it that you haven't talked to him."

"I haven't seen him in more than a week," I confess and immediately feel guilt take up residence in the back of my throat. "If I see him, I'll feel uncomfortable and weird, and it's better if I avoid that altogether."

"Juniper Snow, I've never known you to be a coward." Sarah crosses her arms over her chest, and to my surprise, they both look mad at me.

Like, *really* mad.

"What's this all about?"

"We love you," Luna says. "But we love Apollo, too. You need to tell him. If you don't, I will, and I won't apologize for it. Stop being a chicken shit and just *do it*."

I want to yell at them and tell them that they don't understand and that, at the end of the day, it's none of their goddamn business.

I want that, but it would be wrong because everything they're saying is true.

I *am* being a coward.

"Okay."

They blink at me, look at each other, and then my way once more.

"Okay?" Sarah echoes.

"Yeah, okay. You're right. I hate that you are, but facts are facts. I'll go over to his place tonight and tell him. I don't know how, and I'm super stressed about it, but I know that I need to. So, I'll do it. I've had my time to freak out and think and freak out some more."

"Have you decided what you want to do about the baby?" Luna asks.

"There was always only the option for me, but I had to warm up to it." I pat my stomach, not in the sweet way that most soon-to-be moms do, but in kind of an awkward way that I figure I'll get used to after some time passes. "Whether or not Apollo wants to be included in our lives is really up to him."

"I don't see him running," Sarah says thoughtfully. "I'll be interested to hear how it all goes."

"I'll keep you posted. In the meantime, I have to go to the chapel. The city's coming by to pick up the bodies tomorrow, and I have to go down in the body closet to make sure everything is ready for them. Oh, and Grandma asked me to look for another person. I swear, she should just come over and take inventory herself."

"Did you just call it...*the body closet*?" Luna asks with a laugh.

"It's so much easier than mausoleum." I shrug and turn to head out. "If you decide you need more decorations, call me. Although, I don't think there's an inch in this place that isn't already covered with bows and lights."

"Good luck tonight," Sarah calls out as I make it to the front door.

Honestly, I doubt there is enough luck—good or bad —that will get me through the next couple of hours. On top of getting queasy and light-headed every time I consider telling Apollo I'm knocked up, which has nothing to do with the morning sickness that's been kicking my ass, I have to actually do this favor for my grandmother.

I can't believe that I agreed to go back down to that body closet. When I'm not at the chapel, it doesn't seem like a big deal, but as soon as I get down there, I hyperventilate and break out in hives.

It absolutely terrifies me, and I can't get rid of it soon enough.

"Just get in and get out," I mutter to myself as I park in front of the chapel and walk inside.

When I step through my front door, I forget to be terrified for a moment because it's so *pretty* in here now. Thanks to the hard work of my crew and friends and family in Huckleberry Bay, this space has turned into something new. I can't believe how much progress everyone has made in just over a week's time. The floor is in, the walls are painted the perfect shade of white, which reflects the light from the windows so well. The plumbing and electrical are completely done, and I've spent a little more time than necessary in the bathroom, watching the water run in the faucet. The only things left to finish are countertops and a couple pieces of trim here and there, and I can move in. If I *really* wanted to, I could move in now, but I'm stubborn, and I want it to be completely finished, in every way, before I move in my stuff.

"It's on schedule," I murmur in amazement. Christmas is just a few days away, and my gifts to myself

—some new living room and bedroom furniture—are waiting at the store, ready to be delivered.

I do a little dance before crossing the big space, past my gorgeous kitchen, complete with new appliances and sage-green cabinets, and open the door to the mudroom.

"They even finished *this*."

I'm in awe of the beautiful built-in space to hang coats and stow boots and shoes and bags, and the deep sink that's next to the brand-new washer and dryer. It'll be the perfect spot to walk into after a long and dirty day at work to shed my filthy clothes, wash my hands, and tidy up before walking through the rest of the house, so I keep my mess in one spot, near the back entrance.

The floor of the mudroom is a gorgeous black-and-white mosaic tile that looks fantastic against the same sage-green of the built-ins and kitchen cabinets.

At least this is all done before the baby is even *close* to being here. I won't have to worry about trying to finish my own house before he or she arrives.

With gratitude and love taking up residence in my chest, I pull a deep breath into my lungs and open the door to the basement.

Nothing about this has changed.

"You can do this. It's only a basement."

I flip the light switch and start down the stairs.

"Sure, it's creepy as all get-out, but there's absolutely nothing down here that can hurt me. It's totally fine. Just go in there and look for a Francine Brown who would be about the same age as Grandma, and then get the hell out of here. I'm a badass, and I've got this."

The pep talk doesn't really help, but speaking out loud takes the edge off the silence and helps to soothe me.

Once the heavy door to the body room is open, I step inside and flip on the light. The hair on the back of my neck immediately stands on end.

"Fucking creepy as hell," I mutter, beginning my journey through the room, scanning all the nameplates. "I have to set some boundaries."

"Do you often talk to yourself?"

"Shit!" I turn, my hand on my chest as my heart kicks up into overdrive, and find Eric, the stupid asshole from New York, standing in the doorway. "What are you doing here? This is private property. Get the fuck out of here."

"I came to talk some sense into you," he says as he slowly walks into the room and looks around. "Man, it's pretty fucking creepy down here, isn't it?"

"I want you to leave." I need to keep the fear from showing on my face. Keep my badass attitude in the forefront, and do *not* let him see that I'm scared to death here. If I wasn't pregnant, I'd just kick his ass, but now I have a baby to think of.

"Too fucking bad." His eyes flash as he glares over at me, and I curse myself for not bringing anything down here with me but my phone, which is next to useless as a weapon. He could do anything down here. No one would hear me scream.

Hold it together, June.

I don't say anything as he continues to walk around and then circles back to the door.

I should have walked through that door when he wasn't standing in front of it, and now I can't.

I am *not* holding it together.

"What would you like to discuss, Eric?" At least my voice isn't shaking.

"The property. Don't act fucking stupid. It's not cute."

"I wasn't trying to be *cute*. I just don't see how you have any business asking questions about things that aren't any of your concern. Even if it were, do you really think acting like this is any way to go about getting me to talk to you about it?"

"I think you'll do exactly what I want you to do." He smiles, but it's a sinister, gross twist of his lips that makes a shiver run down my spine. I want him *gone*. "Because if you don't, I'll burn this place to the fucking ground. Literally. I will burn that inn, your grandmother's house, and every other pathetic structure in this godforsaken town that means anything to you. I'll ruin it all."

"Because of a city-block worth of land?" I shake my head. "That's ridiculous. It's not that valuable. There is property in any town up and down the West Coast that you can invest in. This isn't the only place in the world."

"It's the principle of it!" The scream echoes through the room, making me flinch, and the asshole has the gall to look satisfied because of it.

He's nothing but a fucking bully.

"So, at the heart of it, if you peel back all the excuses and stuff, you're pissed because I won." I tilt my head and watch as a muscle in his jaw twitches and his hands ball into fists. "Are you going to hit me, Eric?"

"I want to fucking *kill you*."

It's the absolute truth. I've never seen so much rage, so much hatred in someone's face, and when I remember just how much of a disadvantage I'm at down here, I force myself to relax and adopt an unassuming posture.

"I don't want to sell to you," I say softly, almost apologetically, but it's the honest truth.

"Well, then maybe spending some time in here with the...dead will give you some time to think about changing your mind. Otherwise, you'll end up just like them."

"Wait!"

Before I can reach him, he closes the door, and I hear him lock it from the outside.

"Open this door!" Banging with the side of my fist, full-on panic starts to settle in. I'm locked inside the *body closet* by myself.

I don't even know if air can get in here.

"Please, open this door." I hear the tears in my voice as I start to plead. "I'm pregnant. I can't be in here. Please, open the door."

But the lock doesn't release, and there is only the echoing cadence of my heartbeat in my ears and hollow silence of the room.

He couldn't have really left me locked down here.

My hands start to shake, and my breaths turn into gasps of air that aren't enough to fill my lungs when I start to worry that he's destroying all the work I've put into the living space. I picture him setting my chapel on fire and letting it burn down with me trapped beneath it.

"Oh my god, he's going to burn me up in here." Do I smell smoke, or is that my panicked imagination?

I pull my phone out of my pocket, but there's no service down here. Probably because this room is lined with lead to keep out the moisture.

"Shit." I lean back against the door and stare straight ahead in horror. Hundreds of names stare back at me. "This is my worst nightmare. This, right here."

My breathing quickens, tripping from frantic to hyperventilation, and I can't make it stop. My heart is beating so fast that I'm starting to get light-headed and dizzy, so I slide down the door, pull my legs to my chest, and drop my forehead to my knees.

"Oh, baby," I whisper as the tears come. There's a noise in the back corner that has my eyelids squeezing shut and the tears flowing faster. "I'm so sorry. I'm so sorry, little baby."

I swear that I can hear whispers—actual *voices*—and it scares me so much, that my body trembles uncontrollably.

If I cry hard enough, maybe it'll drown out the scary sounds coming from inside this body closet.

Maybe someone will hear me.

"I didn't even get to tell your daddy about you," I whisper, regret for not telling Apollo swelling like a wave inside me.

What's happening upstairs? Are we going to burn down here? I think I *do* smell smoke.

259

"No. No, we're not going to die."

I stand and start banging on the door again. I know that no one can hear me outside, but if someone comes into the chapel, into the mudroom, they might hear me.

There's more whispering behind me, so I whirl around and yell, "Shut the fuck up! I'm sick of you scaring me down here. You can't hurt me. I forbid it. So, just shut up, unless you plan on getting me out of here."

The room falls silent, and I turn to the door once more, banging and screaming for help.

It doesn't take long before my hands start to hurt, but I bang on the door for as long as I can stand it, but then I realize I'm just wasting energy. I need a plan, and screaming at a locked door is a terrible one.

"No one's coming," I whisper and rest my forehead on the door. "I don't know what I'm going to do."

MAY 1, 2023

DEAR DIARY,

Holy shit, I'm knocked up. Preggers. With child. What in the actual hell am I going to do? I haven't talked to Apollo about it yet. Yeah, it's been a while since I've written in here, and I forgot to tell you that the man that drives me the most crazy in all of the world is the man that I've gone and fallen in love with, I can't stop sleeping with him, and now I'm pregnant with his baby.

I don't know if he'll be exactly thrilled about this.

I'm scared that I'll suck at motherhood, like my mom did. All babies deserve so much better than that. I'm confused, and scared, and probably hormonal. I'll figure it out, I guess.

And I have to talk to Apollo.

Yikes.

XO,

June

Chapter Eighteen

Apollo

After my chat with my father yesterday, I decided to follow his advice and let June take her time to "work through her mad" and then come have it out with me so we can get on with things.

That lasted a whole fourteen hours before I decided that she'd had long enough. I woke up and decided that I was going to find her so we can talk. Sure, I'm frustrated with her, but even more than that, I fucking miss the hell out of her.

I know she's been at Luna's inn quite a lot lately, helping to get the place ready for the wedding next week after Christmas. So, that's where I head first. When I get there, June's truck isn't there, but I cut the engine anyway.

"Damn it all to hell," I mutter as I get out and head inside to talk to Luna, who I find in the kitchen with Sarah and Mira.

"You have excellent timing," Mira says, pulling a pan

of something that smells delicious and sweet out of the oven. "I have fresh cinnamon rolls."

"You know I can't pass that up, but first"—I turn to my sister—"I need to know where June is."

Luna blinks at me, turns to Sarah, who's suddenly grinning, and then back to me.

"She left about twenty minutes ago. She's at the chapel."

I sigh, nod, and turn back to Mira. "Do you mind boxing two of those up to go?"

"You betcha." Mira winks and reaches for a box. "Is everything okay with our June?"

"I'm going to figure that out today." Glancing back at my sister, I take a breath. "I'm in love with her."

"I know." Luna smiles brightly and then hurries over to hug me. "And I'm so happy for you."

"Don't be quite yet. She's not speaking to me."

"She will," Sarah says with way more confidence than I feel. "Take her those rolls and have a chat with her. You'll see."

I narrow my eyes and look at both women with suspicion. "What do you know that I don't?"

"Nothing." Luna blows a raspberry and shakes her head.

"You're doing that thing you do when you lie."

"Whatever." She shrugs, as tight-lipped as she's always been when it comes to her friend. "Cinnamon rolls are her favorite. Go see her."

I accept the box from Mira, who tugs on my sleeve, which is her silent demand that I bend down so she can kiss my cheek. She does, and before I can straighten, she whispers, "Don't leave there until you have your answers."

Then she pats my shoulder and goes back to work.

"Women are weird," I mutter as I walk back out to my truck and head toward the chapel.

Sure enough, June's truck is parked in front.

With the box of warm rolls in my hand, I walk up to the door and, finding it unlocked, let myself in.

"June?"

There's no response to my call, so I walk farther inside and set the box on a stool by the kitchen island.

It looks great in here. Once the countertops are installed tomorrow and the last of the trim is nailed into place, the cleaning crew can come in and get it ready for June. Come hell or high water, my girl will be moved in *before* Christmas morning.

First, though, I have to find her and make sure she's still *my* girl.

"June?" I call out again and poke my head into both bedrooms, the bathroom, and even the small office that June decided she wanted to add.

She's not here.

"Where the hell did she go? Mudroom?" I check, but she's not in there either. "Damn, this is a really nice room."

Suddenly, I smell...*roses*.

It's happened before while I was living at the lighthouse, and even once or twice while I was working at the inn, but I'd never smelled it in the chapel. Rose, the former owner of the lighthouse property, and my I-don't-know-how many-times-great-grandmother, has always been around, but she's never left the lighthouse.

The hairs on the back of my neck stand on end, and I *know* that this is Rose.

"Okay, what are you telling me? Is something wrong?" The scent lightens, and when I walk back to the entrance to the kitchen, it's gone altogether. "Okay, this way?"

I walk toward the basement steps, and the scent of roses grows overpowering.

"Shit, is June down there?"

I fling open the door and run down the stairs. The lights are on, and I know that she wouldn't leave them on if she wasn't down here.

The door to the mausoleum is closed, and I stand in the middle of the room, trying to calm my breathing so that I can listen. After a second, I hear a thump coming from the other side of the heavy door.

"June?"

"Help!" The cry is soft, barely audible, as I rush over and try to turn the knob, but it's locked.

"Jesus, she locked herself in there." I turn the lock, open the door, and a *very* hysterical June spills out into my arms.

"Oh, god." She clings to me, sobbing into my chest. "Apollo."

"Come on."

"Get me the f-f-fuck out of here."

"You got it, baby." I lift her into my arms, cradling her

against me as I walk through the empty basement and up the steps. The smell of roses is dissipating as I take her into the main house, but before I can set her down, she shakes her head violently.

"No, not here. I need to be out of here."

"I'll take you to my place."

Her face is buried in my neck as I carry her to my truck. She doesn't want to let go of me as I settle her in the seat, but I untangle her arms from around my neck.

"You have to let go for just a few minutes while I get us home, okay?"

She doesn't answer, but she does release me so she can pull her knees up to her chin and hold herself in a small ball.

For fuck's sake, what happened to her down there? My first instinct is to demand she tell me what happened so I know if I have to kill someone for doing this to her.

I don't bother to ask her—not yet, anyway—and drive to my place. Once we're there, I go through the same motions of taking her into my arms and carrying her inside.

After sitting on the couch, still cradling her against me, I wrap her in a blanket because she's started to shiver as if she's in shock.

"Baby, you have to breathe." I drag my hand up and down her back, trying to soothe her. "Long, deep breaths now. Listen to me."

She turns her face up so she can see me, and I breathe with her, long and slow. She mimics me, and the shivering starts to subside.

"Good girl. You're safe. Juniper." My hand traces up and down her spine again. "You're safe, baby. I won't let anything hurt you. I've got you."

"H-h-he locked me in." Her eyes well with fresh tears, and the anger that spears through me is swift and all-encompassing.

"Who did?"

"Eric." She sniffs and pulls her sleeve over her hand so she can wipe at her nose and the tears on her cheeks. "Jesus, Apollo, he locked me *in* there with the dead people. They whispered at me, and it was so fucking scary."

"You're safe now. I promise." I take another deep breath, which she mirrors, and then I fish my phone out of my pocket to call Cullen.

"Yo," he says in my ear.

"I need you at my place, now. June was assaulted and locked into the mausoleum in her basement. I found her and brought her here. She's pretty upset, and I don't know the whole story yet."

"On my way." He hangs up, and I toss my phone onto the couch next to us. Silent tears are still trailing down her cheeks, so I brush them away and then tuck her hair behind her ears. "Cullen is on his way. We'll figure this out."

"He's crazy," she whispers and leans in to bury her face in my neck. "And I'm so sorry that I'm a bitch and I haven't talked to you."

"Enough of that." I hug her close and kiss her head.

"We'll talk about that later. Let's handle one thing at a time, okay?"

It breaks my heart to see her so...broken. June is one of the strongest people I know. She doesn't fall apart. She doesn't have panic attacks.

She's as sturdy as they come.

She nods, and just a few minutes later, I hear a vehicle pull up outside, a car door slam, and then Cullen is storming through my front door.

"Hey," I say as he kneels next to June and brushes his hand over her hair.

"June?"

"Cullen." She lets go of me as fresh tears spill down her cheeks, leaning into her brother and hugging him. "Jesus Christ, I'm still so scared."

"Okay, it's okay. Honey, you're fine now." He pats her back and then leans away to look at her face. "Fucking hell, you're white as a ghost."

"Don't say *ghost*," she says, closing her eyes. He and I share a look of concern, but then she firms her chin, takes a deep breath, and lets it out slowly. "Okay, I'm getting it together. I'm going to be fine."

"Who do I have to find?" Cullen asks and then shakes his head. "I'm jumping the gun. Tell us what happened."

"I went down in the basement because Grandma wanted me to look for a person in the body closet."

I raise an eyebrow, having no idea what a body closet is, but I don't interrupt her.

"I was in there, and suddenly, Eric—the asshole from New York—was in there with me. He was *pissed*, talking about how if I didn't sell him the property I just bought, he'd burn down my chapel, the inn, and Grandma's house."

More tears fall, and she impatiently brushes them away.

"He said that if he locked me in there, maybe I'd have time to think about it, and he *did*. He locked me in there, and I knew that no one would be able to hear me scream. I could hear whispers and noises, and it was so fucking *scary*. I'm never going back down there. The city is moving the remains tomorrow, but they don't need me down there."

"No," Cullen says, patting her back. "They don't, and no one is going to make you go back down there. Do you have cameras set up around the chapel?"

June's eyes light up. "Yes! Yes, after what happened with the spray paint, I had cameras installed at all of my sites, including the chapel."

She pulls out her phone, pulls up the footage, and offers the device to her brother. "Take it. There will be footage of him coming in and out of the chapel. Fucking hell, I was so scared. I thought he was going to go upstairs and set the place on fire."

"He was long gone by the time I arrived," I add, speaking for the first time. "I'd stopped by the inn, and Luna told me you'd left about twenty minutes prior. When I got to the chapel, I didn't see you anywhere, but then I smelled roses."

269

June's eyes fly over to mine, wide in surprise. "*Rose* led you to me?"

"She did, and I'm so fucking glad."

"Me, too." Fresh tears want to fall, but June squares her shoulders and turns to her brother. "Can Eric get into trouble for what he did?"

"He'll be charged with a whole host of things, including kidnapping, trespassing, criminal mischief, breaking and entering, and everything else that I can find. He will absolutely have to pay for this."

"I just wanted him to *leave*. I think he has some pretty severe mental health issues."

"That's for the court to decide," Cullen says simply. "I'm going to go over to the chapel and see if anything else was disturbed. We'll pull some fingerprints, because there should be some on the doorknobs, and I'll put out an APB for his arrest. When you're up to it, you'll have to come down and make a formal statement, too. Do you know his last name?"

June nods and gives him the information that she has, including the asshole's phone number, and then Cullen is gone.

"I don't think that I've ever had a panic attack like that," June says, looking over at me. "When you opened that door, it was the biggest relief of my life."

"You scared the hell out of me," I admit and let out a long, shaky breath. "Jesus, Juniper, I love you so much, and I hate that you were so terrified and alone down there."

Her eyes fill with tears *again*.

"What now? Please don't cry, baby. You're safe."

"You *love me*?"

"That's why you're crying?"

She brushes impatiently at the tears. "Do you mean that you love me, or are you just saying that because I'm a sobbing mess?"

"I've told you I love you before."

"No." She shakes her head and stands to pace the room. "You've said that you love everything about the *sex*, but that's different."

"I—" I frown, thinking back. "Okay, it was during sex that I said that, yes. But I didn't mean that I love only the sex. Fuck me, June, is that what you thought?"

"I don't know!" She throws up her hands, still pacing. "I can't read minds!"

"No, but you're really good at drawing conclusions. So, let me spell it out for you, in plain language, when we're not naked and trembling, okay? I love you."

I smile as she stops stomping around and stares at me.

"You make me crazy in the best ways. You challenge me, and you make me laugh. You're so fucking smart that it's a little intimidating."

She snorts, but I keep going.

"Yeah, I love *everything* about you, inside and out. You're sexy as hell, and I feel like I'm alive when I'm with you. Does that explain it clearly enough?"

"I think so." She drops into the chair across from me and clasps her hands together before biting her lip. "I think I've been in love with you since I was a kid. Even then, you irritated the hell out of me, which I'm sure you'll do forever a little, but then I fell in love with you again."

"Wait, I'm doing the math." I make motions in the air with my finger as if I'm carrying the one and then laugh when she kicks out at me. "I'm glad you love me back."

"I have something super serious to tell you," she says and clears her throat. "Something that might change *everything*."

"Nothing will change how I feel about you."

"Hold that thought." She blows out another breath, seeming so nervous that it's making me want to pull her into my lap again so I can hold her.

Instead, I wait.

"I'mgoingtohaveababy."

The words rush out in a quick string. She flings herself back in the chair, and then she covers her face with her hands.

My mouth opens, but no sound comes out.

She's going to have a baby.

"Are you going to ask if it's yours?" The question is muffled, but I'm out of my seat and falling to my knees in front of her.

Gently, I wrap my fingers around her wrists and tug her hands down.

"Come here."

I pull her toward me and rest my forehead against hers.

"If it's not mine, it was an immaculate conception."

This makes her lips twitch. "I mean, some men—"

"This is *me*. This is us, baby."

"Yeah." She drags her fingertips down my cheeks. "You don't look mad."

"Is this why you wouldn't talk to me for the past week?"

"I was trying to get my head on straight. It really knocked me for a loop, you know? When Luna and Sarah came to see me because I was throwing up so much, they made me pee on a stick—"

"Hold up. The girls know?"

She bites her lip and cringes. "Well, yeah. They were with me when I took the test. If it makes you feel any better, they are *really* mad at me for wanting to wait to tell you."

"I don't know that it makes me feel any better."

"Are you mad?"

"I'm...wow, I don't know what I am, Juniper. In the future, you will *not* wait to tell me big news."

"I don't think it gets any bigger than this, so I can agree to that. If you don't want to be a part of this, I understand."

Now, I pick her up, sit her in my lap, and kiss her senseless before hooking her hair behind her ear.

"I'm not going anywhere, babe. Well, I might move into the chapel with you because it's *sweet*."

"Isn't it so pretty? I'm kind of obsessed with it. I have to say, you're taking this really well. After the way you reacted the first time you forgot a condom, I thought for sure you'd be upset."

I kiss her hand and then press it against my chest. "I didn't want something like this to happen without it being your choice. Maybe that's a really naïve thing to think, but—"

"No, I get it, and it's a really sweet thing to say, but sometimes things happen, even when you try to prevent it. I didn't think I wanted kids at all, to be honest. I just assumed that I'd be the fun aunt to Sarah's and Luna's kids, and I was content with that. I'm not convinced that I'll be a great mom, Apollo."

"Why would you think that?"

"I'm not naturally nurturing. I'm not the touchy-feely type, and I think kids should have a mom who wants hugs and kisses and all the mushy things that I just didn't have as a kid."

"You do those things with me," I reply, and her brows furrow into a frown. "You *do*. I mean, you always say we aren't snuggling, but we are, and you don't pull away. Even now, I'm holding you in my lap, and you're not running. You may not be used to showing a lot of affection because you didn't have a lot of it in your household growing up, but that doesn't mean you don't know how to show love to people. I know, without a shadow of a doubt, that when this baby gets here, you're going to be an *excellent* mother."

"How do you know?" It's said in the sweetest whisper I've ever heard.

"Because you love so completely, so *powerfully*, that loving our baby is going to be second nature for you. I'll be there, too. God knows that I don't know what the fuck I'm doing, so we'll just muddle our way through it together."

"Okay." She nods and licks her lips, thinking it over. "I guess that makes sense. We'll figure it out, and I don't have to do it by myself."

"Never." Holding her chin with the tip of my finger, I lower my lips to hers. "You won't ever be alone, Juniper."

Epilogue

June

"We have to go," Apollo whispers in my ear, and I roll onto my back and stretch lazily, absolutely *loving* the fact that we're lying in our bedroom in the finished chapel together.

"I'm so cozy, though," I reply and smile when he kisses me on the nose. "We've lived in this house for less than a week, and I never want to leave."

"I get it, I really do. But if we don't go to Luna's wedding, she'll kill us both, and we'll never come back here."

"You're right." I sit up, letting the sheet fall, and stretch before finally climbing out of bed.

Apollo and I moved into the chapel and had everything unpacked and our Christmas tree set up and decorated two days before Christmas.

I got what I wanted, after all.

"When is Indigo going to put your house on the

market?" I ask as I pad into the bathroom to wash my face and brush my teeth.

"Monday," he replies. "He doesn't think it'll take long to sell."

"You know, you could just rent it out or use it as a vacation rental."

"No." He wraps his arms around me from behind and kisses my cheek. "You're the real-estate-mogul half of this relationship. I'd rather just sell the place so I don't have to worry about it. I'm not attached to that house, and it was more or less just a place to crash."

"Okay. I'm going to walk through those empty buildings over on my new property to figure out if I can restore them, or if I have to tear them down and start over. I think I'll do that tomorrow."

"Not by yourself, you won't."

I scowl at him in the mirror. "You can't boss me around."

"You're pregnant."

"Yeah, not disabled. I'm not even throwing up as much anymore."

"I'm not really comfortable with you walking through there, potentially falling through a rotted-out floorboard and getting hurt, Juniper."

"You're being ridiculous—"

He spins me around, grasps my shoulders, and kisses me *hard*. "I love you, and I don't want you hurt, okay? I'm not trying to be an asshole."

"Kind of sounds like you are."

That makes him grin. "Can we compromise? What if I asked you to take Rob or me with you, just in case?"

"Rob's already on standby to go with me." I laugh when he tickles me. "It's so fun to get you all worked up."

"I'm going to spank you for that later."

"Promises, promises. Okay, I have to go to the inn to get my hair and makeup done. What are you doing?"

"I'm going to Wolfe's big-ass garage where we're going to get ready and play pool and do man stuff."

I roll my eyes and walk back to the bedroom to get dressed in leggings and a button-down shirt, per Luna's expressed orders.

"Please don't get drunk before the ceremony."

"Nah, we'll save that for *after* the ceremony."

"I'm only going to have three mimosas." I have to turn away from him and press my lips together so I don't laugh. I *know* he's staring daggers into my back. "I mean, a few drinks shouldn't hurt anything."

"June."

I close my eyes and pinch my lips closed, refusing to respond.

"Sure, go ahead and have *four* mimosas. Hell, smoke a bowl while you're at it."

"You're no fun." I whirl around and find him grinning at me. "I was trying to egg you on."

"You wouldn't do anything so reckless," he replies.

"Except walk across rotten floors, thus endangering our unborn child."

"You're stubborn." He shrugs and goes to grab his

suit, which is in a garment bag in the closet. "Shall we ride together?"

"Sure, you can drop me off."

I'm excited to spend the day with Luna, Sarah, and a whole bunch of other people who will be in and out during the day. My grandma and Luna's mom are both going to be there, and when those two get together, there is never a dull moment.

The whole town of Huckleberry Bay is abuzz with excitement for tonight's party. Those who haven't been lucky enough to stay at the inn overnight at some point in the last month are anxious to see the finished result. Add in the fact that there's a wedding, and it's as if the air is vibrating with anticipation.

It's going to be a hell of a day.

"Have fun," Apollo says when he drops me off. "Let me know if you need anything."

"I will. You have fun, too. Don't let Wolfe escape and come over here to get a peek at Luna. It's forbidden."

"Yes, ma'am." He winks, and after I close the passenger door, he drives away.

When I walk inside and head upstairs to the bridal suite, I'm surprised to find that Luna somehow managed to have even *more* decorations brought in.

Mostly flowers, but still, it's as if Christmas threw up in here.

"Are you ready for this?" I ask as I walk into the room and pull to a stop. Luna, Sarah, and Luna's mom are already here, getting their hair and makeup done. "You said to be here by *ten*. I'm not late."

279

"No, we just got an early start," Luna says as she smiles and holds her hand out for me. "How are you feeling today?"

"Really well, actually. The worst of it seems to be over." I sniff the air. "I don't smell Rose anymore."

"I haven't smelled her or sensed her since we laid Daniel to rest," Luna says.

"Apollo has." I relay what my man told me about following Rose's scent down to the basement to find me last week. "She helped him. Hell, she might have saved my life. I was so scared."

"So, she's at rest, but she's still on standby in case we need her," Sarah says with a smile. "That's actually really sweet."

"You guys." I bite my lip, not really sure if now is the right time to ask but decide to anyway. "Would you be upset if I named this baby Rose? If it's a girl, that is."

"Oh, my god, I think that would be awesome," Luna says. "And I'd jump up and hug you if she didn't have a hot curling iron pressed to my skull."

"You're sure you don't mind? Rose is kind of *yours*."

"She's Apollo's, too, and let's be honest, ever since the day we found her diary, she's been all of ours."

Relieved, I let out a long breath. "Yeah, okay."

"I think that's maybe the sweetest thing ever," Sarah adds. "I'm so happy, you guys. For all of us."

"Me, too." Luna smiles and looks at herself in the mirror. "Now, let's get this show on the road."

"Ladies and gentlemen, it's my pleasure to introduce Mr. And Mrs. Wolfe Conrad!"

The applause is deafening as the newly married couple makes their way onto the covered patio behind the inn. Everyone they pass shouts well wishes and congratulates them, and I don't think I've ever seen either one of them look so happy.

"That ceremony was beautiful," Grandma says as she comes to stand next to me. She's in a gorgeous, bright red dress that perfectly matches her red-rimmed glasses.

"It really was," I agree. "How are you? Do you need anything?"

"Oh, I'm going to go get some of that delicious food in a minute or so. How are you feeling?"

"I'm fine."

She glances at my drink and then back up at me. "No alcohol tonight?"

I shake my head and feel the smile spread over my lips. "It would be really bad for the baby."

Apollo and I told of our families, officially, that we're together on Christmas. But we've been waiting to break the news about the baby until after my first trimester is over.

This is *Annabelle,* though, and from the look of pure joy on her face, I'd say she's pretty damn happy.

"Oh, my sweet girl." She reaches up to frame my face in her hands. "You're going to be one hell of a mama."

"And you're going to be a *great* great-grandma."

That makes her pause, and then she lets out a loud *whoop!* "You bet your ass I am!"

Hurrying off to tell her friends, I smile at Apollo as he joins me.

"What was that about?"

"Well, get ready for the whole town to know that we're expecting in about six-point-nine seconds because I couldn't keep it a secret from her anymore."

"It's okay. I told my parents." My jaw drops, but he just he shrugs, adding, "They're leaving in a few days, and I wanted them to know before they went home."

"That makes sense, and I know they won't make a huge deal about it in front of everyone, but now that Grandma knows and is likely telling everyone with ears, I'm worried the news might take the spotlight away from Luna and Wolfe. That's the last thing I want."

Worry twists inside me, and Apollo draws me closer, dropping a kiss to the top of my head. Slowly, I relax, and my attention slides to my best friend and her husband.

"God, they're so disgustingly happy." They are sitting at their table, leaning close and laughing at something only they know about. Apollo laughs. "Why does that gross you out?"

"It actually doesn't, but I have a reputation to uphold, you know?" I don't pull away when Apollo takes my hand, links our fingers, and pulls them up to his lips so he can kiss my knuckles. "I'm not even trying to deck you for doing that in public. See? I'm improving."

"Your self-control is awe-inspiring." He winks when I narrow my eyes at him. "So, speaking of weddings, what kind do you want?"

"What kind of what?"

"Wedding."

My eyes fly up to his, and he's just watching me, waiting for my answer.

"Who said we're having a wedding?"

"I did." He leans in and presses his lips to my ear. "You'll get your ring later when my giving it to you won't steal any thunder from the newlyweds, but you're marrying me, Juniper. I don't want to have to live without you."

"That's so...*sweet?*"

"Also, I love you," he adds. "We can discuss it all later."

I take a deep breath. "I don't think you'll ever stop annoying me *and* disarming me at the same time."

"Probably not."

We quietly watch the crowd for a moment before I look up at Apollo. "Small, by the gazebo, over next to the lighthouse."

He raises an eyebrow.

"That's the wedding I want."

"Then that's what you'll have."

I nod go back to watching our friends and family, feeling grateful for this community of people that I was lucky enough to be born in to. Grateful that I'll be bringing my *own* baby into the same community, where they'll be loved and welcomed.

There's nothing like Huckleberry Bay anywhere else in the world.

And I'm so glad it's mine.

Newsletter Sign Up

I hope you enjoyed reading this story as much as I enjoyed writing it! For upcoming book news, be sure to join my newsletter! I promise I will only send you news-filled mail, and none of the spam. You can sign up here:

https://mailchi.mp/kristenproby.com/newsletter-sign-up

Also by Kristen Proby:

Other Books by Kristen Proby

The With Me In Seattle Series

Come Away With Me - Luke & Natalie
Under The Mistletoe With Me - Isaac & Stacy
Fight With Me - Nate & Jules
Play With Me - Will & Meg
Rock With Me - Leo & Sam
Safe With Me - Caleb & Brynna
Tied With Me - Matt & Nic
Breathe With Me - Mark & Meredith
Forever With Me - Dominic & Alecia
Stay With Me - Wyatt & Amelia
Indulge With Me
Love With Me - Jace & Joy
Dance With Me Levi & Starla

Also by Kristen Proby:

You Belong With Me - Archer & Elena
Dream With Me - Kane & Anastasia
Imagine With Me - Shawn & Lexi
Escape With Me - Keegan & Isabella
Flirt With Me - Hunter & Maeve
Take a Chance With Me - Cameron & Maggie

Check out the full series here: https://www.
kristenprobyauthor.com/with-me-in-seattle

Single in Seattle Series
The Secret - Vaughn & Olivia
The Scandal - Gray & Stella
The Score - Ike & Sophie

Check out the full series here: https://www.
kristenprobyauthor.com/single-in-seattle

Huckleberry Bay Series

Lighthouse Way
Fernhill Lane
Chapel Bend

The Big Sky Universe

Love Under the Big Sky
Loving Cara
Seducing Lauren

Also by Kristen Proby:

Falling for Jillian
Saving Grace

The Big Sky
Charming Hannah
Kissing Jenna
Waiting for Willa
Soaring With Fallon

Big Sky Royal
Enchanting Sebastian
Enticing Liam
Taunting Callum

Heroes of Big Sky
Honor
Courage
Shelter

Check out the full Big Sky universe here:
https://www.kristenprobyauthor.com/under-the-big-sky

Bayou Magic

Shadows
Spells
Serendipity

Check out the full series here: https://www.
kristenprobyauthor.com/bayou-magic

The Curse of the Blood Moon Series

Hallows End
Cauldrons Call
Salems Song

The Romancing Manhattan Series

All the Way
All it Takes
After All

Check out the full series here: https://www.
kristenprobyauthor.com/romancing-manhattan

The Boudreaux Series

Easy Love
Easy Charm
Easy Melody
Easy Kisses
Easy Magic
Easy Fortune
Easy Nights

Check out the full series here: https://www.

Also by Kristen Proby:

kristenprobyauthor.com/boudreaux

The Fusion Series

Listen to Me
Close to You
Blush for Me
The Beauty of Us
Savor You

Check out the full series here: https://www.
kristenprobyauthor.com/fusion

From 1001 Dark Nights

Easy With You
Easy For Keeps
No Reservations
Tempting Brooke
Wonder With Me
Shine With Me
Change With Me
The Scramble
Cherry Lane

Kristen Proby's Crossover Collection

Soaring with Fallon, A Big Sky Novel

Also by Kristen Proby:

Wicked Force: A Wicked Horse Vegas/Big Sky Novella
By Sawyer Bennett

All Stars Fall: A Seaside Pictures/Big Sky Novella
By Rachel Van Dyken

Hold On: A Play On/Big Sky Novella
By Samantha Young

Worth Fighting For: A Warrior Fight Club/Big Sky
Novella
By Laura Kaye

Crazy Imperfect Love: A Dirty Dicks/Big Sky Novella
By K.L. Grayson

Nothing Without You: A Forever Yours/Big Sky Novella
By Monica Murphy

**Check out the entire Crossover Collection
here:** https://www.kristenprobyauthor.com/kristen-
proby-crossover-collection

About the Author

Kristen Proby has published more than sixty titles, many of which have hit the USA Today, New York Times and Wall Street Journal Bestsellers lists.

Kristen and her husband, John, make their home in her hometown of Whitefish, Montana with their two cats and dog.

facebook.com/booksbykristenproby

instagram.com/kristenproby

bookbub.com/profile/kristen-proby

goodreads.com/kristenproby

CPSIA information can be obtained
at www.ICGtesting.com
Printed in the USA
BVHW040307190423
662580BV00002B/5